For Sydney and Daphne
who were in it
at the beginning

STORMY HERITAGE

STORMY HERITAGE

Mary Williams

WA
200849062V

WILLIAM KIMBER · LONDON

First published in 1987 by
WILLIAM KIMBER & CO. LIMITED
100 Jermyn Street, London, SW1Y 6EE

Typeset by Scarborough Typesetting Services
and printed and bound in Great Britain by
Biddles Limited, Guildford and King's Lynn

1

On a misty evening in 1850, a woman dragging a girl by one hand made her way to the front entrance of a large house looking towards the Bristol channel in a select residential district of Plynport.

The child was slight and small, dressed in a dark cloak and bonnet; her face, in the fitful lamplight, had a pale wisht look. The woman also was thin to the point of gauntness. But as she lifted her head to the mellow glow spilling from windows down the terrace steps, her features were shown to be clear-cut and bold, with high cheek-bones emphasised by rouge and fiery eyes above determined mouth and chin. She walked purposefully, jerking the child ahead every few yards or so as though this mission — whatever it might be — was of utmost importance.

There was little traffic about, and few pedestrians. A hansom cab passed with the muffled clippetty-clop of horses' hooves. From the distance came the mournful echo of a siren across the river, and as the odd couple mounted the steps their shapes became mere shadowed silhouettes in the thickening air. At the corner of the road a top-hatted figure paused uncertainly before deciding to cross to the opposite pavement.

The whole scene had the atmosphere and uncertainty of an impressionistic painting, and except for the woman's decisive tug at the bell-pull, she and her charge could have been beings from some other sphere. Their presence in that well-bred area was somehow out of place, insidiously suggesting localities of another order — of back doors, dockland perhaps, or sinister twilight regions of doubtful pursuits.

Less than a minute passed before the massive door opened. There was an obvious slight argument with the manservant, then the two figures were ushered inside the house. The door closed, leaving only a recess of deeper shade blurred through an intensifying veil of fog.

And that precise moment marked a change in the whole course of Priscilla Clinton's life.

*

From a bedroom window of No 7 Seagrave Square, Priscilla the only daughter and child of William and Lady Elizabeth Clinton, stared down upon the unexpected visitors. The woman, she thought, had the appearance − despite the dim light − of someone applying for a job, in which case she should have gone to the servants' entrance. On the other hand, she had an urgent air about her that was almost intimidating.

The child was so smothered by the unbecoming bonnet and long black coat that any real glimpse of her face was impossible from above. But Priscilla's reaction was instantly defensive. It was as though during those few moments when the figures mounted the steps, her occasional peculiar ability to sense forthcoming events flooded her with apprehension. The fear, this time apparently without reason, was formless and entirely lacking physical basis. But it was there. She knew in a brief second's intuition, that the child was to become in some intimately strange way, a part of the Clinton household, heralding changes that would not be for the better. She left the window abruptly, trying to shake off the unpredictable unease, sighed, went to her mirror, and surveyed her reflection dispassionately, wishing as she did so often those days that she looked older, more grown-up.

She was almost eleven years of age, cream-skinned, with a pair of clear grey eyes framed by dark thick lashes in an oval face that might in maturity be called heart-shaped. Her mouth was too wide for conventional beauty, uptilted at the corners above a small firm chin; her hair, of a subtle sable shade, fell thick and straight down her back. Because it was her mother's birthday she was being allowed to dine with her parents that night; her governess, Miss Perrot, would shortly appear to see she was presentably attired in her best olive green satin gown, which had lace cuffs, and a collar to match, reaching high to the neck above a fitted bodice and full-flounced skirt also edged with lace. She was not yet considered old enough to wear the newer fashionable frame of a crinoline for which she was thankful. The tightness of the bodice was bad enough to bear, and truth to tell, she was not really looking forward to the celebration. Her mother, Lady Elizabeth, had complained of a megrim all that day, and at such times her temper was inclined to be short, casting a gloom over the household.

There was, in fact, little rapport between Elizabeth and her daughter, unlike the young girl's relationship with her father which on her part had from her earliest memory been one of open adoration. Dear Papa! so warm-hearted and amusing, so handsome with his flashing dark eyes, springing black curly hair, and thick sideburns. Often she wondered how he could stand Mama's moods and megrims — or her coldness. Yes, beautiful as Elizabeth might be in a delicate, imperious way — she was after all the daughter of an impoverished lord — Priscilla found it difficult, really impossible, to imagine the couple in bed together making love. And yet they must have done sometimes, or *she*, Priscilla, wouldn't have been born, would she? Just *exactly* what happened between two people in the intimacies of the marriage bed, she didn't know, but she had gathered from snatches of conversation overheard from servants, that it could either be highly enjoyable or something slightly revolting of which one should be ashamed. She knew, of course, that people who loved each other had to be very close together to make a baby — the story she'd been told as a very little girl that only a doctor could bring one in his little black bag, was just not true. But what *exactly* did grown-ups do together? And why was it such a secret business.

Only recently she'd put the question pointedly to Miss Perrot, and the answer had been, 'You must not be so inquisitive. Remember, curiosity killed the cat—'

'But I'm not a cat, Miss Perrot.'

'—and don't interrupt. When the time comes you will find out all about it.'

'How, if no one tells me?'

Miss Perrot's face had turned a deep pink, and she'd sighed between her teeth, making a little clicking sound.

'One day, quite soon perhaps,' the good lady, said after a portentous pause 'or it could be later — no-one can say — something will happen to you, something that all young girls have to go through, and this will be a sign that you are on the way to becoming a young woman. After that, when you're old enough, you'll be able to marry and have children of your own.'

'But—'

'And no buts if you please, miss. You've had my final word on the subject. If you worry me any more, I shall inform her Ladyship, and you'll be punished.'

'I'll ask Papa then,' Priscilla had said defiantly.

'If you do, he'll be very annoyed, quite outraged, and wonder how he ever came to have such a vulgar-minded daughter.'

'I'm *not* vulgar. I—'

'Then don't behave as though you are. I'm sure you don't wish your papa to think badly of you.'

This had silenced Priscilla. Of course she didn't. Papa was her idol, the one person she truly loved in all the world. So she made herself abandon the vexed question temporarily. But she *did* occasionally wonder why it was that most married people had more than one child, yet she had no brothers or sisters although her papa appeared so fond of all young things. It must be something to do with her mother, of course, and her megrims. And probably this was the reason, also, for his sudden unpredictable moods that either took him out of the house in the evenings when Lady Elizabeth complained of being tired, or sent him to his study to busy himself with business papers and books. Priscilla sometimes wondered what went on behind the curtained windows of other houses in that fashionable square. Did other papas and mamas have long silences between them, like hers did? Perhaps not.

Once, when Elizabeth had been particularly irate with her for some small offence and sent her to her room, her father had come up to see her later and said in rich-voiced, conspiratorial tones, 'Take no notice, sweetheart. Just be a little more careful. You must remember that your mama isn't like ordinary folk. She's a *lady*! — an *aristocrat*.'

Had his voice been just slightly bitter? No, it couldn't have been because the next moment he was smiling, and his dark eyes had the well-known mischievous gleam in them when he added, 'Not like you and me, darlin' — we're ordinary folk, and must make allowances.'

'What's the difference between being ordinary and an aristocrat, papa?'

'Ah! Well, a good question.' He'd stroked his thick, short beard, and answered thoughtfully, 'Common clay like you and I know how to enjoy ourselves, that's *one* difference. And work. If it wasn't for the workers where would the money come from to give our betters what they want? Not that the highly born *are* any better. That's the rum part of it. But they *think* they are. And that breeds a whole heap of foolish notions.'

'Well, I'm glad *I'm* not an aristocrat,' Priscilla had said, cuddling up to him. 'I want to be just like *you*. Always.'

'Thank your stars you can't be, my love. You're half-mama and half-papa, remember. That makes you—'

'A mongrel, like Mrs Jolly.' Mrs Jolly was Priscilla's pet dog, half-terrier, half-spaniel.

'No. Just unique, meaning a bit above class distinctions.'

The whole subject had sounded confused and bewildering to Priscilla. Anyway if being 'unique' was what her father wanted, then she was content for it to be so, and during the days that followed the problem of babies had been replaced by far more important matters in her mind including that of her future, when she was to go to boarding school. The thought, though exciting, was depressing to her, but because mama wished it, it appeared there could be no alternative. She would be packed off to some strict, boring place where lots of other girls like herself would be taught the rules of being prepared for the social life of a well-behaved young lady, whatever that meant. She would wear a uniform, she supposed, like the girls of a

11

school on the outskirts of the city, and there'd be no fun at all. No cosy chats with papa, or secret sessions in the kitchen where she was spoiled by Mrs James, the cook. Just 'yes, miss,' and 'no, miss', and having to embroider and stitch hems without getting pricks of blood on the linen, recite dates and silly verses and practise long scales on the piano. Oh, it would be horrible.

But there would be no escaping it, because despite Lady Elizabeth's vagueness and delicate health, once she had made up her mind on any course of action she invariably had her way. And this time it would be the same; papa might object at first, and be on his daughter's side, but in the end he'd give in, because he so hated scenes.

If only mama had truly loved her, Priscilla thought frequently, everyone would have been so much happier. Once, as a very small girl she'd longed and tried in every way to win Elizabeth's true affection, but there'd been no warmth of response. Mama was too aloof and icy. Even when she'd kissed the child or praised her on occasion for being a good girl, it was as though some lofty goddess had descended for a brief moment from Olympian heights to grant a favour, then off again, with a majestic lift of her lovely head on its swan-like neck, and a swirl of silk gown and petticoats leaving a drift of exotic perfume behind.

They were so unalike, that was the trouble. Wherever Priscilla went, excitement and vitality seemed to flood the air. Her youth itself and vibrant voice, quick movements, alternating moods of unpredictable sadness and wild joy, jarred Elizabeth's highly wrought nerves.

'She's such a *tomboy*,' she'd complained more than once to her husband. 'So − *restless* somehow.'

'Well, my dear, what did you expect when you married me? A little angel? A plaster saint? Good God, Elizabeth, she's just a *child*. Can't you let your corsets out once in a while and unbend a little?'

'Don't be coarse, William.'

'Coarse?' He'd laughed shortly. 'I have coarse roots, which have been very effective on your behalf in providing the wherewithal for your luxurious existence. It might be as well for you to remember it sometimes.'

Following this dry observation Elizabeth had retorted, 'In your way you know you are quite a snob, William.'

'*Me?*'

'Yes. So proud of your humble beginnings you can't resist a chance of airing the good use you've made of them. Well, I wish you wouldn't − not in front of Priscilla at least. Children are impressionable. When she's older her background will be an important stepping stone to her future. She's so stubborn. Sometimes, I really believe she takes a perverse pleasure in thwarting any ambitions I have for her. Oh − I'm sorry. I'm not trying to rub things in − the differences of family I mean. I do *admire* how you've got on, William—' Her eyes had momentarily and briefly softened. 'But—'

'The fact remains I rose from humble origins; apprenticeship to junior surveyor, then site-engineer, and builder of bridges resulting in an undertaking that finally put me on the map by some, as second only to Isambard Brunel. Quite commendable, you must agree, but *trade*. *Trade*, Elizabeth.'

She'd flushed faintly at the implication. 'There's no need to be sarcastic, William, or imply I married you for your money.'

'I'm quite aware there was more to it than that − at the beginning. And I did my damnedest to make you happy, give you all you wanted. I couldn't though, could I? Not in the end. *I* failed *you* in sensibility and class, just as *you* failed *me* in not giving me a son. That makes us quits, I think. So let's be honest and friendly about our relationship as much as possible − for Priscilla's sake, if not our own.'

'I'm not aware of having said or done anything to lessen your image in our daughter's eyes,' his wife had said coldly. 'In fact, I've always upheld your opinion over any problems in her upbringing. She'd devoted to you, which is more than can be said of me. Sometimes she appears positively to dislike me.'

'You're exaggerating,' he'd retorted curtly. 'As I said, if you could only unbend, soften a little—'

'Oh, really, William! What *are* we arguing about? It's all so senseless.'

'I agree.' He'd turned on his heel sharply and walked to the door. 'I may be late tonight, so don't wait up for me.'

The door closed with a snap, and he'd gone before she could say more. Off to his club, she supposed wearily or some other haunt of his where he could relax in his own way, freed of her company. She had no illusions about her husband. The earthy vitality that had impressed and deluded her before and during the early days of their marriage, had long since demanded escape channels from their relationship, and she had come to terms with the situation, recognising that those very qualities in him which so exhausted her — his robust attitude to life, tremendous energy and acute business mind allied to a constructive imagination — had enabled him to amass the considerable fortune she now enjoyed.

She never pried or questioned his male activities away from home, accepting only what she wished to know. That he worked to excess was understandable, and so long as the 'front' of their marriage was sustained agreeably to the approval of society and the world, she made no outward complaint. That her existence had become emotionally sterile she realised but would not admit, resorting to pills or potions to alleviate her constant headaches and 'megrims' as her husband termed them.

There were times when inward resentment churned — resentment at her own inability to appreciate William's bluff and adventurous attack on life. Over food, for instance, though not a glutton, he was certainly a gourmet, whereas, with the passing of years, it was all she could do to delicately pick at a small portion of chicken breast taking a minimum of the essential etceteras to make it at all palatable. Yes, her zest for existence had faded, leaving not the nobly born delicately nurtured and lovely girl he had married, but a woman regally poised when the occasion warranted, able to imbue the Clinton household with a modicum of awe, yet inwardly fearful and shrinking, tense from thwarted desires and unfulfilment of a beauty sensed but never realised. Only in her private boudoir could she exhibit a degree of her somewhat 'precious' taste, through priceless Crown Derby china and Coalport figurines – exquisite miniatures and soft pastel silks and brocade furnishings, finely woven Persian rubs in subdued rich shades of blue, rose, and deep purples intermingled with gold. The furniture was mostly elegant gilt of the Louis Quinze period, and the air of the particular sanctum was fragrant always with pot-pourri and her personal subtle perfume.

Birthdays, she thought on that auspicious occasion which was to herald such dramatic changes in the household, were a bore after forty; there was no pleasure for her having to face the fact that she was now forty-two. Studying her reflection through the oval mirror of her dressing-table, a brief glow of satisfaction pierced the shadow of the lingering headache. The blue-grey chiffon gown was complementary to her clear pale skin and honey-gold hair. And the red rose dutifully presented to her that afternoon by William, and worn at her bosom, seemed to intensify the faint glow on her high cheek bones. Yet still she did not feel the pleasurable anticipation one was supposed to on a birthday. And her back, though so straight, ached. She *did* hope her husband wouldn't be too vociferous or determinedly charming. There would be champagne, of course, which didn't really mix well with the potion she'd had to take earlier. But William would persist in her having at least one glass, and take the opportunity himself of having three or four.

Until the last few years, he had insisted, on each occasion of the celebration, in an excessive display of manly eroticism in the bedroom later. Thank goodness all that was over now, she thought reminiscently. Looking back fleetingly she recalled the effort it had been not to shrink from his sexual exuberance. At the same time it occurred to her with mild surprise how *very* rarely nowadays he cast even a desirous glance in her direction. Still, it was surely better that way, and dinner that night would probably pass peaceably enough.

But she was wrong.

Five minutes later, to her surprise, she was informed by a servant that 'the master' asked to see her in the large parlour.

15

'I shall be down for dinner presently,' Elizabeth exclaimed. 'Surely any gifts or particular preliminaries can wait—?'

'Mr Clinton was very definite, m'lady,' came the answer, before she could finish. 'It's not exactly — there are two *persons* with him, madam.'

Her fine eyebrows arched.

'*Persons?*'

'A woman. And a child.'

'*Really!* How very extraordionary. Guests, do you mean?'

'Oh, I shouldn't think so. Ordinary-looking, if you understand me, madam. Not your kind at all.'

Elizabeth frowned.

'Very well. Tell Mr Clinton I'll be down almost immediately.'

There was a click of the door followed by the receding sound of footsteps.

What on earth had William been up to, Elizabeth wondered irritably? And *why* must he allow her to be bothered at such a time by an unwarranted intrusion into what was after all a very personal event.

The niggle of her headache revived again. She sighed, touched a curl tentatively that had strayed from a comb about her temple, reached for her silk embroidered shawl lying over a chair, and with a whisk of perfume and rustle of silk skirts over the voluminous chiffon, went to the door where she stopped for an instant, almost forgetting her fan which most probably would be needed. Then, with her head held high she made her way down the wide staircase and crossed the hall to the parlour.

*

Priscilla was surprised when Miss Perrot came briskly into her room and informed her that she needn't hurry downstairs, indeed, that she must not, because dinner would be at least half an hour late.

'But why? Papa said I must be just a bit earlier so we could be there before mama, ready to greet her. Has the meal gone wrong or something? Cook isn't ill, is she?'

'Now, now. Not so many questions. Compose yourself, child.

16

Certainly cook's not ill, nothing of the sort. And there's nothing wrong. Just a slight interruption. You must—'

'*I* know. Those people I saw — I—'

'Don't interrupt. You're letting your imagination run away with you. Later, if there's anything that concerns you, you'll hear about it from your papa, or mama herself, perhaps. In the meantime, you could do a little reading, or occupy yourself with your sampler — *providing* you're careful not to prick your finger. Having to put in an extra rosebud where that small spot of blood had been didn't improve the design at all.'

'I don't want to do stuffy embroidery,' Priscilla said, defiantly, '*or* read. I'm — I'm—'

'Yes, miss?' Her governess's tones were grim.

'I don't know. Nobody tells me anything,' the child retorted miserably.

'Perhaps because you ask all the wrong questions. Matters not suitable for a child of your years.'

'How do I know what's suitable and what isn't?' Priscilla demanded, 'And I'm not a baby, Miss Perrot. Nearly eleven. In — in India and places like that girls are married then.'

'You're not an Indian,' her governess snapped. 'If you were you'd certainly have been disciplined into behaving better before your elders. I really don't know what's got into you lately. No wonder her Ladyship gets headaches.'

'What do you mean?'

'*Miss Perrot* if you please. Remember your manners.'

'Miss Perrot,' Priscilla echoed. 'I'm sorry.'

'Thank you. And what I mean, young lady, is that your mama frequently worries about you, and I'm afraid has cause to.'

'Oh, *fiddlesticks*.'

'*What* did you say?' Miss Perrot's face and voice were equally outraged.

'Fiddlesticks — *fiddlesticks*. I'm so tired of being preached at, and I don't believe mama worries about me at all. She doesn't care about *anything* except her appearance, and pills and potions and smelling salts, and being haughty and a *lady*. Well,

I'm not a lady like you called me. I'm *me*, myself. And papa understands. He's the only one who's kind and doesn't blame me for what goes wrong — except Cook perhaps. Cook's nice, and Ted, the stable boy. Yes, I *like* Ted. P'raps—' She paused briefly before adding with a wicked glint in her eyes, 'P'raps I should have been born a stable girl. Are there stable girls, Miss Perrot?'

For some moments after the outburst Miss Perrot did not reply. Then in an outraged breathless voice, with her thin chest heaving indignantly, she said, 'Never in my life have I witnessed such a disgraceful show of bad manners and impertinence from any child under my tuition. If it was in my power to do so, I would severely chastise you. Yes, a beating is what you deserve. As it is I shall report you to your—'

'Papa? Ah! but he wouldn't listen. Well, he might pretend to, but I know he'd be on my side really.'

With a great effort Miss Perrot controlled herself to say with only a slight tremor in her voice, 'No more arguing, if you please. Pull yourself together, comb your hair properly, and push that stupid strand from your forehead, or shall I do it for you?'

'No Miss Perrot, thank you,' Priscilla answered, with a sudden show of assumed meekness. 'I'll do it myself.'

'And are your hands clean?'

A display of upturned palms showed that they were.

'Very well,' the governess said. 'And don't forget your mittens. I shall leave you now, to consider your behaviour, and when I return shortly I shall expect to find you contrite and tidy, and ready to join your mama and papa in a polite frame of mind.'

With starchy hauteur the thin figure marched to the door, went through and slammed it sharply behind her before hurrying down the corridor to her own premises.

Priscilla relaxed, giving a faint giggle. Then, just as quickly her expression changed to solemnity. Poor old Perrot, she thought, almost with sympathy. It must be awful always having to give orders and be responsible for her charge's learning and good manners, especially anyone like herself who could be so thoroughly *bad* on occasion.

She didn't really *wish* to be wicked but she knew she was. Not in any terrible way, of course — she never wanted consciously to hurt anyone, or anything in the world, not even her stonyfaced governess. Only Miss Perrot was so very boring; and life shouldn't be boring, it *shouldn't*. There was so much to love and get excited about, given a chance, especially in the springtime when the air was heady and sweet and wild, and the old apple tree in the garden foamed white with blossom.

The autumn was nice too — or *could* be if she was allowed to go out on her own, racing with the brown and gold leaves driven from the trees on a salty sea-born wind. But she never had the chance, except on *very* rare occasions when papa found an excuse to take her on some vague 'business outing' contrived for the satisfaction of Miss Perrot and mama. And when she went to boarding school — *if* — things would probably be much worse.

As it happened, the 'if' became a far more debatable factor concerning her future on that very evening of Lady Elizabeth's birthday and the arrival of Lise.

Dinner was delayed not for a mere thirty minutes, but for almost an hour. During that time of waiting, and between Miss Perrot's intermittent visits to her bedroom, Priscilla moved restlessly about, trying to concentrate on a book one moment, the next jumping up in exasperation, going to the window overlooking the shrouded night. Lights sprinkled the distant river and city.

She wondered what Dockland would be like now. Once or twice she had driven there with her father and found the twisting cobbled streets and fishy smelling alleys exciting. But it had been daytime then. The small secret-looking cafes would be lit up at this hour. Sailors and foreigners and those painted-up strange looking women she'd heard the servants refer to as pross-something-or-other would be lingering at street corners or laughing behind the rosy glimmer of inn-windows. She'd like to be there, that's what she'd like, so she could write it all down in her little book. The book no one knew about — not even her papa. Oh yes, that's what she was going to be one day — she was going to be a writer. Not like Miss Jane Austen who only wrote about well-bred people — she knew enough about them from Miss Perrot and her mama — but colourful, flashing-eyed dangerous people, and poor ones too, the kind that came into papa's category of workers. Oh! there was so much to find out and discover for oneself.

She sighed heavily and went to the door, paused a moment, then pressed her ear to the crack, and keyhole.

From downstairs there was a confused sound of murmuring and footsteps, followed by that of doors opening and closing. They'd gone, Priscilla thought. Whoever had delayed dinner had now departed. She walked back to her dressing table, and stood there meekly poised, waiting for Miss Perrot. But she didn't come for some time. How odd. On impulse Priscilla returned to her listening post. Everything was still and silent except for a subdued hint of argument, followed by a funny muffled kind of noise that could have been mama in distress. Then the soft pad of footsteps across the hall registered, and what sounded like the closing of the drawingroom door. The footsteps died gradually down the passage to the servants' quarters, and all Priscilla could hear was the ticking of the old grandfather clock on the landing.

Miss Perrot returned at last, and told her charge she could now join her ladyship and the master. Her eyes had a narrowed look, her lips were closed forbiddingly. Priscilla was dying to ask what had been going on, but recognised the futility of doing so, and after enduring a quick tug by thin fingers at her lace collar presumably to straighten it, allowed herself to be ushered down-stairs into the vast dining room.

Presents, including a large bottle of expensive perfume, were arranged on the sideboard. The hatch was open, and Lady Elizabeth was already seated at one end of the shining mahogany table facing William Clinton, who was standing at the other end, with a glass in his hand, and champagne ready uncorked for the celebrations. A servant placed Priscilla's chair in the right position while her father forced a bluff greeting. But his daughter was not deceived. Something was wrong, very wrong. William's over-red face had a twitch at one temple, and Elizabeth's eyes had a strained puffiness of the lids suggesting extreme exhaustion or that she had been crying. Her smile though wide, was thin and taut. There was no warmth in the atmosphere. It was – in the words of the old adage – '—as though you could cut it with a knife'.

The falseness of the conversation, the tension between two adults striving to present a veneer of affability meant to deceive their daughter, depressed and bewildered Priscilla to a point of acute nervous and physical discomfort. She wanted to jump up and rush from the room, run somewhere with Mrs Jolly her dog, and roll in the heather or race along the seashore five miles away, safe from the rules and restrictions and bickering of grown-up folk. She couldn't, of course. It was night-time, autumn and too far away. She'd just have to sit up straight on her chair and pretend to be enjoying the tasty food, while her parents made polite stilted remarks to each other and her mama toyed with entrées that were too rich, she said, for her delicate digestion, and would probably mean she'd have a disturbed night.

Papa, Priscilla noticed, was drinking more wine than he usually did at other festive occasions. His speech too was slightly slurred, and although he smiled frequently at his daughter, his expression when it rested on his wife was moody and sullen.

Oh dear! Priscilla thought again. Something very serious must be wrong. Why weren't they open about it and tell her what it was? After all, she wasn't a baby. And they had no-one else of their own to share things with.

At one point, she almost blurted out the question, but was restrained by Lady Elizabeth's ringing for her maid to fetch her reticule. 'I need my smelling salts,' she said coldly in response to William's sardonically raised eyebrows. 'This room seems particularly airless tonight.'

After that, Priscilla's initiative and courage failed her. She would wait until tomorrow. Tomorrow she'd somehow get papa on his own, and he'd confide in her.

But as it happened in the morning she didn't have to ask and thre was no need to bother her father. Quite soon after breakfast she was summoned to the parlour.

And then the truth was revealed.

She knew.

*

Elizabeth and William were standing at opposite sides of the fireplace when Priscilla was shown into papa's private study. A fire glowed from the grate, outlining their figures which for a few seconds stood motionless as though carved in stone. Then William with a gesture of one arm said in gruff commanding tones very unlike those he generally used when addressing his daughter, 'Come in, come in, child. Your mama and I — hum — have something important to tell you, something I hope will give you pleasure eventually.'

He paused, twirled one end of his moustache and continued, 'The fact is, my dear, in future you will have companionship. From today there will be another girl — slightly younger than you — but only two years, and two years is not much — to share your lessons and our family life. She — her name is Lise, and she is my ward.'

There was a brief silence in which knowledge, with the impact of a pistol-shot, pierced Priscilla's quick intelligence. The girl, she thought suddenly, swiftly and with a sense of doom, the drab-looking shadowy small form glimpsed the other night on the steps of the house, she was the one. At the time Priscilla remembered she'd experienced one of her queer forebodings — that uncanny feeling of something unpleasant ahead which more often than not had proved correct. She'd put it to the back of her mind, but it had happened all the same. It was true. And she was fiercely resentful. She said nothing; just stared at her father for a few seconds in disbelief while he lowered his head slightly, peering at her through slightly narrowed lids, waiting for her reaction.

'Well, Priscilla?' she heard her mother saying with a high grating note in her icy well-bred voice. 'You heard what your father said. His *ward!* which means she is to have all the privileges of a sister. It will be quite an experience for you, will it not? And for us all, I'm *sure*.' Her tones, though controlled, held a sarcastic bitterness, almost venom, which did not escape her daughter. Priscilla noted Elizabeth's rigid demeanour for the first time. The cold, still slightly red-rimmed, eyes, and set of mouth, the look of dislike turned suddenly on her husband.

'Do *you* want her here, mama?' the child asked. 'And why is she papa's ward?' Her clear eyes turned to her father. 'Why, papa?'

'She has no one else now to turn to. So I have to accept the responsibility. After all—' he made a great effort to assume an attitude of bonhomie '—we may all have quite a jolly time together. Once we get used to the idea.'

'I don't think I shall get used to it,' Priscilla said in definite, unchildlike tones. 'And why should I pretend to be happy? It's the girl I saw last night, isn't it? With that funny woman—'

'Priscilla!' her mother interrupted sharply. 'What you or I think is of no importance in this matter, which your father has already demonstrated quite – unequivocably – to me. You've heard what he's just said; she's to take her place in this house as a relative – a foster sister, or—'

'A sister sounds simpler,' William interposed quickly, 'and why you have to be awkward about it, child, I don't know. You'll have companionship, and if you've a mind for it, will be able to help.'

'How?'

'With her lessons, and games; and let her share Mrs Jolly—'

'*No*. I won't let anyone share her.' Tears against her will, were gathering thickly at the back of Priscilla's throat. 'She's *my* dog. Why should I? And lessons – I'm going to boarding school, aren't I? That's what you and mama have been planning for ages. So what's the use of *me* helping to teach *her* – because that's what it would be—'

'You may be mistaken,' Lady Elizabeth interposed drily. 'To me she appeared quite bright, in a certain way, when we met last night. Indeed, even slightly sophisticated. As for boarding school, your papa may decide it is not the best course for you after all. You know, ultimately, that any important decision rests *entirely* with him, so we shall have to wait and see. Now—' she turned away with a sigh of fatigue, or it could have been boredom '—I've really had enough of this conversation, William, so—'

'Yes?' He spoke curtly, throwing an angry sidelong look at his wife.

'Don't you think it's high time you introduced your − ward − to our daughter?'

William went to the door, opened it, and called, 'Miss Perrot, bring the child in.'

A minute later the governess appeared with a hand on the slight small figure's shoulder.

'Come along, my dear,' she said in her friendliest voice. 'There's no need to be frightened—'

Frightened? Priscilla thought, seeing the newcomer's face clearly for the first time. *She'd* never be frightened. Why should she be? She was the most beautiful girl she'd ever seen in her life, and the most spectacular, with a mass of fair hair, so pale and shining it appeared almost silver-white, framing a delicately tinted heart-shaped face and long-lashed eyes above an intriguingly tilted little nose and perfectly formed mouth. In contrast to the silver-gold hair the eyes were brilliantly dark, as dark even as papa's, and the effect was quite dramatic. She was wearing a blue gown, not the one she came in obviously, but one of Priscilla's. It was too large for her, but the bodice had been taken in and a white sash tied at the back emphasised the small waist.

Priscilla's first reaction was of shock, then envy, followed by the grudging thought that here indeed was a rival. Papa always had a fondness for beauty; suppose he grew to love her more than herself? Oh, it *couldn't* happen, it mustn't. She glanced at his face quickly before he spoke. His expression said nothing, but his eyes were fixed on Lise as though he could not tear them away. Then suddenly, he gave a short laugh, stretched out an arm and said, 'Welcome, my dear, for the second time. This—'

24

indicating Priscilla 'is my daughter, and your—' He swallowed before continuing '—Shall we say sister by adoption?'

The little girl said nothing. 'Well, well,' William remarked briefly, 'we needn't be too particular about the relationship. Your name's Lise, and a very charming one; easy on the tongue. Priscilla, love, haven't you a word of greeting?'

'Hullo,' Priscilla remarked grudgingly.

'Bonjour,' the ethereal-looking little creature lisped.

'Oh, lord yes! I forgot,' William said. 'She speaks French better than English. Brought up there, y'see. Useful in a way, don't you think so, Elizabeth? To learn each other's language, eh?'

'I've no thoughts on the matter at all,' her Ladyship answered, 'and if you'll excuse me now, I'll retire. I have a headache. I'm sure Miss Perrot is capable of taking charge from now on.'

Yes, thought Priscilla defensively, and she'd be all fussy and full of praise for the intruder. They would speak French together, and she, Priscilla, wouldn't know what they were talking about. She'd never learned the language properly, although her governess, to do her justice, had tried to teach her. Just odd phrases like *'Je t'aime'*, *'donnez moi la plume'*, *'merci, madame'*, and lines from the song *'Sur le pont d'Avignon'*, things like that. Oh, this pretty-pretty Lise was going to make life more boring than ever. There'd be no fun, she knew it, because already the newcomer was staring upwards at papa like an angel, making him fiddle uncomfortably with his cravat. Not that Lise was *really* like an angel. How could she be, with those large brilliant eyes and pouting red lips?

So from the start the two children became, in a sense, opponents in an emotional dramatic battle. During the days that followed Priscilla tried hard at times to befriend her new companion, simply because papa had urged her to, on more than one occasion. But it was painful to see how William was beginning to dote on Lise, and how Lise, in her turn, so warmly responded. Lady Elizabeth to the contrary, retired more and more to the seclusion of her boudoir, and it soon became known to the whole household that William and she no longer shared the connubial bedroom. Priscilla was quieter and more equable with her mother now than she had ever been, because she was sorry for her, and sensed that behind her chill restrained exterior she suffered.

If only mama and papa could be brought closer, Priscilla thought often, Lise's disturbing influence would be lessened. But there seemed no way of broaching the subject. She was on the point of bringing the subject up one day when she found William alone in the conservatory. But his expression on hearing her voice saying 'Papa,' made her desist. He appeared so tense, strained and unsmiling. 'Well, my dear?'

'I wondered — couldn't — oh?' she broke off, confused. 'It doesn't matter. It's nothing.'

She turned to go.

'Priscilla.'

'Yes?'

'I hope you're getting on better now with Lise. She's such a shy, gentle child.'

Priscilla wanted to cry, 'She isn't shy at all. She's just quiet and sneaky. She's no good at lessons either — she doesn't learn properly or even want to. *That* wouldn't matter, *I* don't care. But all she thinks about is looking nice and making people like her. Even Perrot. Perrot's gone all soft about her. Well, it's Lise's fault. She even puts up her face to be kissed. *Kissed*, can you imagine it, the sly creature. I don't like her, papa, there's something queer about her, and I *hate* having to share her bedroom. Why should I? It was my place before. And now even Mrs Jolly doesn't come there. Because of her'.

Yes, a whole train of resentment struggled in her for outlet, but just at that moment she sensed more harm than good could come from uttering it. So after listening to another plea from her father, she left him to his own thoughts and departed.

However, in the January of the following year the thing Miss Perrot had referred to concerning her developing maturity when she would become a young woman happened, and although it was a shock at first, Priscilla was profoundly grateful, because it enabled her at last to demand the right to have her bedroom to herself again.

2

By February of 1851 Priscilla had become accustomed to the presence of Lise in the Clinton House, although inwardly envious still of the attention evoked by the child's beauty. With Miss Perrot, though the new pupil's capacity for absorbing learning was dull, she remained in favour, due to her charming veneer and perfect manners which Priscilla found unnatural. There was a subtle allure about her that went strangely with her delicate air of innocence, and times when a sidelong glance from her very dark eyes under the long lashes, indicated an instinctive sophistry far from childlike. Cook was one of the few who doubted she was half so trusting and innocent as she appeared to be. 'She has a "knowing" streak in her, that one,' she remarked to Alice, the head housemaid, one day. 'I'd like to know where she come from and how the master came to be responsible for her. To *my* mind—'

'Yes?'

'Oh well, enough of gossip. The little thing seems friendly enough, loving you could almost say. Too loving by half. No wonder Miss Priscilla's jealous. The master seems to dote on her and before she arrived young Prissy was his darling. What the end'll be goodness only knows. As for her Ladyship! — hm. From the look of her if she carries on the way she's going, she won't be long for this world.'

It was true that Elizabeth day by day appeared to be drawing further into her own private world, keeping mostly to her own apartment, and seldom dining downstairs. The servants whispered among themselves that she was forever supping from the sherry decanter, or having a glass of her own particular liqueur brandy purchased secretly for her by her personal maid, unknown to William, from a local inn a quarter of a mile away. Yet she was extremely careful, on the occasions when she ventured downstairs, to show no sign of inebriation. Only a skilled observer might detect that her poise was a trifle too perfect, her speech too calculatingly defined and stilted to be quite natural. If there was any aroma about her person, when she was summoned by William on rare occasions to meet an unexpected crony of his, it would more likely be of peppermint than the exotic perfume of earlier days. She would then teeter perhaps very slightly on the tips of her elegantly shod feet, but her poise would be graceful, and aloofly polite.

William, of course, was shrewdly aware of his lady wife's increasing failing, and was irritated, not because he grudged her her little pleasures, but because he felt in some way guilty, and recognised that the cause lay with him — his inability any more to wish marital contact, though in heaven's name, he told himself frequently, she had been the first offender in that respect — and the fact that he had brought Lise into their home. The last straw, in Elizabeth's eyes, had been when he'd insisted that the lovely fairy-like little girl should be endowed with the Clinton surname.

'Only fair,' he'd stated, 'and simpler. Much simpler. Two Miss Clintons instead of one, eh?'

Elizabeth had turned away in disgust. Although her pride in the past months had forbidden her to ask outright if her robust and virile husband had sired the child, commonsense told her it was far more likely he had than not. She just did not wish to hear it from his own lips. It was the same in the kitchen. Knowing glances had been thrown between the servants during Lise's first weeks there, and still were, at intermittent intervals whenever reference was made to 'the master's ward'.

Once even Priscilla's attention had been caught by a giggling allusion to 'Lise, that pretty little bastard', when for some unknown reason she'd paused outside the kitchen and listened, and there'd been a 'shush' from someone, probably the cook, the firm tread of feet and opening of the door, revealing the broad form and face of Cook considerably flushed, with beads of moisture about her forehead and upper lip. The other servants were either about their work or had disappeared into the dairy or sculleries.

'Well, Miss Priscilla love, did you want anything?' Mrs James asked. 'A biscuit or a slice of cherry cake? Hm?'

Priscilla had shaken her head. 'No thank you. I was just thinking—'

'Yes? What about? Come along now, tell me.'

'Oh, nothing,' Priscilla had answered, feeling slightly confused, because she knew 'bastard' wasn't a nice word, and had something to do with shame and people not being married. 'I was having a think,' she'd added quickly.

'Oh? And what about, love?'

'Just lots of things.' And this had been quite true. 'I can't explain now. One day I will, but not now. You see it's a secret.'

The conversation had ended there. Priscilla had skipped away and up to her bedroom where 'the secret', a notebook, was lying in a drawer under some neatly folded clothes.

She'd taken it out and regarded it solemnly for a few moments before sitting on her bed with a pencil in her hand.

Then she'd started to read. The title was written in capitals by her own hand, considerably larger than the rest of the childishly formed script. It was the beginning of her very first book intended to be a novel and was called *The Gipsy and the Guinea* or *The Adventures of Robert Tyzackass*

The opening ran:

The evening was grey and thundry and filled with gloom, when Sir Robert Tyzackass rode on his black stalyon down a wandring Cornish lane. Sir Robert was the son of a lord. He was very hansome and wild looking and was dressed in a red coat and tall black hat. He was going to be marrid the next day to Lady Dorabella Starch. She wasn't bewtiful, and Sir Robert wasn't happy, but she was rich and Sir Robert's father needed money, so it had all been arranged. When the big stalyon reached a corner a gipsy girl jumped out from the hedge and said O sir, please a penny, we are so poor and needing food.

Sir Robert felt in his pockit for a coin and flung her a golden scented guinea. She checked it and said thank you sir, o thank you. She had long black hair, and red lips, and her eye-lashes were so long they swept her cheeks.

Sir Robert felt a pang cluch his heart. He fell in love with her in a flash. I can't marry Lady Dorabella Starch, he thought in angwish. What am I going to do?—

The writing ended there. Priscilla looked puzzled as she laid the notebook down. The spelling was wrong in places. She wasn't so good at spelling as making up plots. She'd have to look up the dictionary for some of the words. Miss Perrot always told her she should use her head and study grammar more before attempting any serious composition. Well, perhaps it was true. But to Priscilla it was getting the story down that was the most important and she wanted very much for her very first novel to be dramatic and inspiring. Sir Robert Tyzackass, for instance, must be terribly attractive and commanding; the kind of hero who would sweep a beautiful girl off her feet and face all kinds of dangers for her sake. Now what would he do in this case? She chewed her pencil thoughtfully. There was the old lord too, and his money problems. But first of all she had to concoct some brave deed to make everyone who read the story long to meet someone like him.

I know, she thought, a fight. There could be a gipsy man who was jealous and who'd spring out at Sir Robert with a dagger in his hand, but Sir Robert would overcome him without having to use his pistol, and put the beautiful gipsy girl on his handsome steed, and ride away with her to the coast where they'd find a boat and take off for foreign lands. Smugglers and brigands might attack them, and the father of Lady Dorabella Starch would swear vengeance against Sir Robert for deserting his daughter. Lady Dorabella would wait weeping at the altar and be so distressed she'd swoon. Oh, so many exciting things could happen. The difficulty, for Priscilla, was in having time and being free enough from Lise to write the story unknown to anyone else. This problem in itself with other minor adjustments in the routine of running Number 7 softened the resentment she felt at having to share her father's affection; a relief also. One of the *good* things that had accrued from the advent of Lise, was that the boarding school project was shelved. The children, William told his wife quite peremptorily, should not be parted at the commencement of their home life together.

'Lise wouldn't fit in at any organised establishment,' he'd stated. 'Her upbringing's been so — well, damn it all, Elizabeth, you can see how neglected her learning's been. She'd feel inferior, especially with Prissy being so bright, and shoved into a much higher form probably.'

Her Ladyship's hand shook slightly, as she said, with more than a hint of her old tartness, 'I was not aware you were so engrossed or au fait with the education of the young, William. But, of course, this one — the little changeling — is a special case, is she not?'

'Now there's no need to get testy, old girl—'

'And don't you dare, don't you *dare* to call me old girl,' Elizabeth retorted with her lovely face taking on an unbecoming rosy hue. Indeed, her husband thought, with an unusually perceptive glance at the fine features that had once so intrigued him, his lady wife was no longer quite the elegant-looking highly-bred creature he'd taken for granted since their marriage. The realisation was somewhat discomforting.

Why couldn't she accept facts more pleasantly, he wondered irritably. Lise no doubt had been a bit of a shock to her. For that matter, you could have knocked him sideways for six at first, when Annette had produced her that autumn night. Like a ghost from the past she'd been, except that ghosts didn't have flesh and blood in them and eyes so uncannily brilliantly dark like his own. Oh, he'd known from the start that she was his. There'd been no doubt in him. And Annette! Whatever her faults, she'd never been a liar. Poor Annette! He'd have pitied her if she was the sort to need pity. But she wasn't, never had been. Fierce as a tiger, provocative and hard, proud of her

31

profession so long as she could command a good business-like price for what she had to sell. Had she cared for Lise at all properly, as a mother would? Probably, or she'd never had bothered about her future and the tedious journey to Britain from France.

'Not long to live,' she'd told him, 'as you can see for yourself. But this one—' indicating the child, 'she's got a right. I'm not asking for money this time.' She'd laughed shortly, raspingly, put a handkerchief to her lips where a streak of crimson trickled, and continued when she'd got her breath back, 'Nothing to sell any more. But you'll take Lise, yes?'

Shocked, he'd noted in the flickering glow of candles and fire-light the hollowed cheeks under the prominent bones, the brilliance of her eyes through the paint and powder, the thin chest from where each breath taken came with a rattle and odour of sickness.

Shame had gnawed him, not because of that far off night when Elizabeth's coldness following the birth of Priscilla had driven him to seek comfort in a foreign brothel, but shame that life could wreak such havoc with a body that had once been so full of vitality and allure. He had felt no contrition on Elizabeth's behalf. He was no libertine or ever had been in the accepted sense. But the tremendous vitality and creative urge that had made his name famous as a pioneer engineer and designer of vast schemes throughout the country had demanded in rare leisure moments the natural physical outlets and relaxation of any normal healthy male.

His relationship with Annette Lefage had been so brief as to be almost forgotten during the following years. He had not known of any daughter, but instinct, and a knowledge of Annette's character, a down-to-earth honesty and her inherent French capacity to assess and handle facts in the most practical possible way, had been sufficient proof to him, when she'd presented the child on that autumn night. The eyes, too, Lise's eyes, which were also his own. From the first moment of recognition, he'd known what he must do, had recognised also Elizabeth's resentment, but not entirely calculated the extent of it.

Neither had he fully realised, and still did not quite, what he was taking on.

During the young girl's first days in his home the compassion in him had been warm and overflowing, full of plans for both her and Priscilla that had temporarily blinded him to the excessive ardour of the child's response. There was never an occasion, in his company, when she didn't fiercely, passionately, take every opportunity to reach out to him, her gaze ablaze with a desire for love that he gradually began to find embarrassing. Her looks were those of some beautiful sprite — a fairy child. But her manner, the ardour expressed, was that of an adult. There was in her character, despite her youth, a subtle, haunting sexuality that warned him she would later have to be watched — a quality far in excess of other traits or virtues she might possess. Mentally she was not bright. He soon came to realise this, as did Priscilla, and certainly Miss Perrot. But the latter had become so infatuated by the little girl's charm, beauty, and quaint manners of speech, that she denied the sorry fact, even to herself, and when questions were asked at lessons she more often than not put the answer subtly into the child's own mouth, prompting her by such remarks as 'What you mean is, so and so,' or giving whatever reply was needed with '. . . isn't that right, Lise?'

And when Priscilla gave a scornful glance towards the bewildered child, the governess would turn rigidly towards her and remark sharply, 'You see, Priscilla, Lise is learning very quickly. Soon, unless you try harder, she will be ahead of you, and that would be most regrettable, would it not?'

'Yes,' Priscilla would answer automatically, thinking how stupid her governess was to believe she could be deluded by such a silly statement.

The consequence inevitably of shared education between two children of such unequal talent, one slightly simple-minded, the other older and over-bright, was to the detriment of the latter, a fact that even Lady Elizabeth during the rare sessions she had with her child, discovered. So one evening, having resolutely refrained for once from bemusing herself with alcohol, she went downstairs and accosted her husband in his study.

Immediately, on her entering, he got up from his chair, pushed the papers he'd been dealing with aside, and said, 'Elizabeth. How unexpected. May I ask to what I owe this very unusual pleasure?'

'I shan't keep you, William,' his wife replied in controlled tones. 'My complaint will be brief.'

'Complaint?'

'It's about Priscilla. I had a conversation with her yesterday, and it appears her education is not progressing as it should. She is bored. *Bored*, William, because that − that girl you brought in has no brain at all for any kind of learning. Her mentality is below standard, which you yourself should have noticed had you not been so besotted by her looks and sly French manners.'

'Elizabeth—'

'No. Hear me out. You *shall* listen, William, because it concerns your own daughter born to us in legal wedlock. I know you've always been passionately devoted to her, and that she feels the same towards you. Or *did*.'

'Did?'

Elizabeth stared at him with a look of rigid contempt on her haughty face. 'You don't expect her to *continue* loving you, do you? When your preference and thought for that little − bastard − are so evident?'

William's face flushed. The fingers of one hand bit into his palm. 'I will not hear that word spoken in my presence, madam. Do you understand? Certainly not when referring to one of my family.'

All the thwarted anger and lack of courteous consideration Elizabeth had endured during the last few years, surged to the surface of her being as a wave of acute indignation which broke from her lips in vituperative passion.

'You, *you*! You will have this, you will *not* have that. You − *you*. Always *you*, isn't it? The great William Clinton?' She smiled an uncalled for acid-sweet smile, paused and continued more conciliatorily. 'No doubt you have a remarkable talent for impressing your names on bridges and buildings. But have you ever considered establishing a harmonious home-life or conceding to *my* wishes on occasion?'

Her mastery of words and manners momentarily silenced him, then he answered coldly, 'Anything in reason you've asked for you've had—'

'*Anything!* William, did you woo me with gentle words, even during our courtship? Did you give a single thought of the shock it might be to a young girl — I was only eighteen — suddenly married off to a—'

'Common working man,' he interrupted darkly.

'I didn't say that. But you made no attempt to *adjust* either culturally or physically. It was *I* who had to do that. Oh, I realise it never occurred to you. Beyond possessing me, your dreams were all of bricks and mortar. But I was flesh and blood, William. I knew nothing of life. I was *goods*. Married off.'

He stared at her shocked. Never before had she spoken to him so openly, almost brutally.

'I — well, I — I took it you loved me, or at least had a fondness,' he remarked. 'You certainly appeared to have—'

'Duty, William. It was my duty.'

The statement fell from her lips with a curious chilling sadness.

'Then damn it all—' Anger rose in him that this lily-cold woman could possess still such a power to mortally wound him. 'You knew what you were doing, didn't you? And I'm quite sure, Elizabeth, your saintly show of self-sacrifice is mostly bunkum. Yes, *Bunkum*. Anyway—' he stared at her resentfully, noting that although too thin by half, she'd lost not a shred of the graceful elegance that was her heritage, '—now we're talking of duty, I don't have to point out to you, I suppose, that you've been pretty clever in evading yours recently for a considerable time, maritally speaking.'

She flushed.

He shrugged. 'Not that it matters any more. A man like me with things to do in life has better ways of spending his time than chasing shadows. Fact is, my dear, the softness I had for you once is gone. Dead as the proverbial dodo. So we're quits, eh? But Priscilla! she's a different matter. Young, warm, my own flesh. I wouldn't—'

'*And* mine, William.'

His mouth took on an odd twist. 'Yes, strange that. Because frankly, my dear, I can't see a trace of resemblance — anywhere.'

'I don't expect you to. You've never tried to find any. No time. All the same, as my daughter — and yours — I do expect you to consider her welfare at this point. It isn't right for her to be cooped up with a totally unsuitable companion who can as yet neither read or write coherently except in bad French, and who is obviously destined for an extremely doubtful future. Her presence here must have caused comment socially already; you may not mind your *own* name being gossipped about, but Priscilla should be removed to a proper environment as soon as possible. Think about it.'

'Is that all?'

'Surely I've said enough. I feel quite exhausted. Talking to you is like—'

'Talking to a brick wall.'

She gave a soft ironical laugh.

'I sincerely hope not, this time.'

As matters turned out, Elizabeth discovered later in the week that it hadn't been.

*

After considering the mutual problem of the two girls' education, William grudgingly formed the opinion that his wife's perspicacity had proved to be correct, and that Priscilla's normal brightness and uninhibited attitude to himself had dimmed during recent months. She seemed withdrawn and frequently showed a preference for her own company, spending more time in her room or in the gazebo at the bottom of the garden than sharing with him the few leisure moments he could spare.

'Are you happy, Prissy, my love,' he asked one day, 'having

36

lessons with Lise? You two get on well together, I hope.' He had found her coming from the arbour walking to the house. She shrugged, looked up at him for a moment or two, then glanced down at her toes. He noticed she was carrying a notebook with a pencil dangling from it.

'Well?' William persisted, 'Is anything wrong? If so, tell me and we'll see what can be done.'

Priscilla sighed, picked a leaf idly from a bush and stood quite still before she said, 'Lise is all right, I suppose. She's funny, but it's not her fault. It's just—'

'Yes?'

'She's so *stupid*, papa. She can't do sums, she can't read, not even *French* properly, and in history we have to say dates over and over again, when I know them all. We *never* get the story part, and when old Perrot asks us questions about *anything* she smiles and nods and tells Lise what to say, then tries to make out how *clever* she is. Lise, I mean. Well, she *isn't*. The only things she knows are—' She broke off realising there was no way of explaining the curious bits and pieces of her past life that Lise had divulged – things that Priscilla hadn't heard of before, and certainly didn't understand.

'Well, child? Go on, such as—' William prompted.

'Oh, nothing. Nothing important or really true, I'm sure they couldn't be. You see, papa, there really is something odd about her – about Lise. I know she's pretty, *you* think so too, don't you? And that's another thing. I can't bear the way she cuddles up to you and lifts her face. She just wants to be petted all the time, and honestly I hate it. Yes, I do. P'raps after all it would be better for me to go to boarding school. I wouldn't have to spend such dreary hours listening to Perrot's soft-soapy voice, and Lise pretending to understand all, gooey-eyed, and Oui, mademoiselle. Mais oui. Oh *merci*!'

William was silent for some moments. Then as they walked on, he said, 'I would rather you two children weren't entirely separated. It's important to *me*, very, that you should form some kind of friendship. But I see now how difficult it is for you to be held back because of any short-comings, or incapacity to learn that Lise may have. Yes, I should have discovered this before. Still, luckily it isn't too late.'

'You mean I *will* go to school?'

'Not exactly, pet. But certainly there must be an entirely different arrangement here. Just leave it to papa. I'll think something out. Be patient, though, for a little time. Well? Will you do this for me?'

Priscilla nodded slowly. 'All right.'

'After Easter, when we return from Mooncarn, we'll have a new beginning for you two girls. *And* for Miss Maud Perrot.'

'Do you mean you're going to send her away, papa?'

'Oh, no, no, no,' he answered. 'As she seems so fond of Lise there'd be no point in doing that. My concern's for you, Prissy. Now no more questions. Just trust me.'

'I'm *glad* we're going to Mooncarn,' Priscilla said with sudden exuberance, recalling their family holiday home on the Cornish moors not far from the sea. 'Will mama come too?'

'I sincerely hope so,' William answered, although his statement was not strictly true. He could no longer picture his lady-wife braving the wild salty winds which in late March and early April so often swept the cliffs and rugged coast. At one time when he'd first bought the old house, she'd professed a certain pleasure in wandering about the twisting byways of Wynk, the nearest village. She'd been fascinated by the main cobbled street leading steeply down to the small harbour, and basked in the admiration of natives and the few holiday-makers, mostly artists, who always gave a second or third glance at the slender figure moving so gracefully in their midst, a faint smile on her lovely face, her hair honey gold under her parasol. She could have been a fragile ethereal figure painted by Millais or Ford Maddox Brown, wearing gauzy, voluminous gowns of muslin that floated on gentle spring breezes giving an ethereal quality against dream-like Cornish blue skies.

Looking back, William realised he'd given more attention to her during that period, thus feeding her vanity and enhancing any romantic feeling she might have had for him. Perhaps he should have tried more, helping to sustain her fragile dreams.

But practicality was at the hard core of his being; he'd always known that to achieve his greatest ambitions dedication to work must be unswerving and relentless. When their first child, a boy, had been stillborn, Elizabeth had changed, become sharper-tongued and more critical, with frayed nerves that had gradually caused the rift between them. She had never been a sexual woman, so—

At this point of retrospection he forced memories aside, dwelling of a necessity on the present, and dedicating his attention the more fiercely to his constructive abilities – to buildings and the creation of the vast projects that were to bring him widely acknowledged fame. He'd been well-known, with quite an enviable fortune behind him when he married Elizabeth. Ten years later, through single-minded initiative, his wealth had increased fourfold. And he still had dreams ahead. A certain canal was on his agenda, a sewage scheme up north, a new bridge linking Cornwall and Devon, and designs had already been accepted by a steamship company for an immense ship of almost thirty tons powered by paddles and screws. Railways and ships – more and more they were absorbing his mind. Not even Priscilla had the power to distract him when he'd once set his will on a business project.

Nevertheless, at regular intervals he made sure all was going well with his household. The problem of Priscilla and Lise was a bit of an obstacle; never before had he seen his beloved firstborn so serenely withdrawn. But then, neither had he the remotest idea of her own secret undertaking, or that but for Sir Robert Tyzackass she would indeed have been at that period a most unhappy child.

As it was, wilfully shutting the everyday world of number 7 Seagrave Square to the back of her brain, Priscilla continued to pen her hero's adventures to paper. She had already altered the title of *The Gipsy and the Guinea* to *Passionate Love* after looking up the correct spelling for 'passionate' in the dictionary. The first chapter, ending with Lady Starch weeping at the altar, had been called 'Escape to the Wilds', underlined and written in block letters.

'. . . Through the wild night the lovers rode', the second episode ran.

The gipsy girl's hair was streaming, and Sir Robert's heart was thumping in his brest. What have I done he thought and what will happen to poor Dorabella. But I can't help it. This is true love. He thumped his steed, and just then a dark figger leaped out from some bushes. He was a highwayman, and related to the gipsy girl's father. Ha, ha! he roared, grabbing the rains, got you now, you wicked cur. He was a very evil looking man, like Satan. His eyes flashed fire, and there was a dredful fight. The highwayman had a pistol but Sir Robert in a flash nocked it out of his hand. I am a *Tyzackass*, he shouted, so I will win. And he did. A moment later his enemy was lying on the ground pleeding for mercy. With a contemptu-us kick of his shining boot Sir Robert said, get up and begon fiend, and never let me see thy fowl countenance again. Then he jumped on his snorting stallyon, and they were off again . . .

At this point, Priscilla had been forced to break off because she hadn't quite made up her mind about the eloping couple's destination. Eventually, she decided on them finding an empty ruined cottage on the wild Cornish coast near Land's End, where they decided to hide, until Sir Robert could find a preacher ready to marry them. 'And the cottage could belong to a smuggler,' she thought, 'where all sorts of stolen jewels and brandy could be hidden.' This idea was so exciting, leading to so many daring adventures, her head seethed, and she began more and more to admire the dashing Sir Robert Tyzackass who in some ways even overshadowed her beloved papa.

Through those days of bewilderment over the strange situation concerning Lise, William and Miss Perrot, she found herself more and more immersed in her fictitious character. The evolving story became a kind of second life to her, a refuge where her emotions could freely go their own sweet wild way unrestricted by the rules and arguments of adults.

However, shortly before Easter she was informed by William that after the holiday she would no longer have to endure the boring sessions with Miss Perrot, but would study under a tutor — a young man who had been destined for the Church and University, but after taking his degree had decided after all that teaching was more to his fancy.

'So you see, my dear,' William said, smiling warmly, 'you'll have every opportunity for learning that you could wish for. Miss Perrot will remain as governess to Lise, while you'll be able to stride ahead in your own way.' He paused, then said, 'What do you think about it, eh?'

Priscilla didn't reply at once, and when she spoke her answer was guarded. 'Will this — this tutor man want me to be religious all the time, papa?'

'My dear child!' William laughed heartily. 'What a hope! Even if he did he'd soon learn better, I'll be bound. No, I've met him, and found him not only clever but highly amusing when he felt like it.' William suddenly changed his mood and became serious. 'Priscilla, love, I'm sure you'll prefer being at home with mama and me rather than going away to school, won't you?'

'With *you* yes. Of course,' Priscilla agreed suddenly, her face lighting up. 'But I wish — I wish mama was different. I mean she's gone strange lately, hasn't she? She was always kind of quiet, and like you said, a lady. But since Lise came she's different. Do you—' She was on the point of asking, 'Do you still love her, papa?' But at the sudden remote cold expression crossing William's face, she changed the question quickly to, 'Is she coming with us to Mooncarn, papa? Mama, I mean?'

'I doubt it,' William answered drily, 'and you must try and understand that your mother isn't strong. She hadn't been well lately. We must make allowances. It's the same with you and your new — companion. I very much want you to be nice to her whenever possible.'

'I will,' Priscilla promised. 'As much as I can.'

The subject was closed there. Life continued in its usual pattern except that William flung himself with renewed energy into his business affairs. *The Adventures of Sir Robert Tyzackass*

41

were temporarily laid aside in the excitement and hubbub of getting ready for the holiday. Miss Perrot became fussily occupied in seeing that the children's clothes were suitably selected and in order. Useful gowns were chosen with plenty of flannel petticoats, warm capes and bonnets if the weather should be cold. Hems were let down for Priscilla, and one or two dresses she'd grown out of adjusted and taken up for Lise. There was no reason for such economy, of course, and Lady Elizabeth on one of her 'good days' suddenly became impatient and paid a visit by chaise to the most select costumiers in Plynport where she purchased in Miss Perrot's secret opinion the most ridiculously extravagant and fancy gowns for the two girls.

William was pleased and complimented his wife on her initiative. 'I'm grateful,' he said.

'What for?'

'Showing an interest again in our − children,' he replied boldly.

'In Lise you mean?' She laughed shortly. 'I'm sure I've always insisted that Priscilla should be attractively clad, and I would hardly leave out the − your ward, since she is now so close a member of the family.'

Disregarding the sarcasm, William persisted, 'Nevertheless, I say again, I'm grateful. Thank you.'

A fortnight later the family entourage set off for Mooncarn, travelling the twenty miles westwards by a railway line, 'The Clinton Special', constructed to William's design. It had been completed only the previous year; the journey therefore was quite an occasion. The party included William himself, one of his men, Jenkins, Miss Perrot, Cook, a kitchen-cum-parlour maid and the two girls. It was William's intention only to stay for the first four days. He had an important business meeting in Plymouth concerning designs for a new large schooner commissioned by an enterprising steamship firm. A problem had arisen concerning fuel consumption which he felt should be more fully debated before plans proceeded.

Priscilla was disappointed when she learned how short his stay would be, but at her first glimpse of the old house again nestling in a fold of the moors, with the glitter of sea in the distance beyond the cliffs, her spirits rose. A rush of excitement seized her, heady as the wild spring winds and scent of heather. She *loved* Mooncarn, its windy paths and tumbled boulders, the standing stones of ancient Celtic days, and only a mile away the tiny village of Wynk nestling above its harbour where fishing boats and a few long-liners bobbed on the water.

The house itself stood in a fold of the moor sheltered at the back by abruptly rising ground spattered in spring by bluebells, primroses and patches of flaming gorse. Small stone-walled fields made a patchwork pattern below, before fading into the giant line of forbidding granite coast. The landscape at intervals was dotted by small farmsteads and occasional dark shapes of mine stacks sending coils of curling smoke to the sky. Above all reigned the immense carn itself, a mysterious relic of unknown history which in certain lights appeared as rugged guardian of its own wild territory. The area, indeed, was of curious ancient significance. At a lower level, beneath the carn, a broken circle of standing stones had given rise to various legends though its true source was unknown.

When William had first bought the house, Mooncarn, it had been in a sad state of neglect, half-ruined. But his discerning mind had instantly seized upon the possibility of restoration, and having for his own something of unique character and use. Intensive research had indicated the building had most probably originated as a large seventeenth century farmhouse built in the popular style of that period round a great chimney stack, in Cornish granite, with a porch set between a pair of gables. The gables he conceded might have been added at a later date, when the farm possibly had become the property of a country gentleman. Whether or not this was true was of little importance, since either design represented the style of the day.

With his creative instinct fully aroused, William had set about rebuilding where necessary, while retaining the original character of the place. Minor adjustments and certain additions had been made, a carriageway to the high moorland road leading to Wynk constructed, and a portion at the front, facing seawards, cultivated as a garden. Ancient cedars still stretched their dark spreading branches towards each other from side to side, thick with glistening foliage, like giant lovers forever pledged to Nature's domain. As if sensing life reborn and vitalised, birds of a wide variety, including doves, wood pigeons, gulls, tits, finches, thrushes, and hooded crows, even an owl, found sanctuary in the territory, shelter from gales which so frequently swept the surrounding wilderness of open land beyond Mooncarn's gates, with ever the taste and lure of freedom when storms had passed.

Only half a mile away was a farm, Trencrowse, hidden round a bend, and reached from Mooncarn by a path curving upwards round the point of a gully, and down again. A narrow cove lay below. From high ground Wynk harbour was visible. Priscilla, who since earliest childhood had known the locality and loved it, was anxious soon after their arrival to fetch milk from the farm and have a word with the Craze family who had the property and a hundred surrounding acres, mostly for sheep and a few cows on life-leasehold.

'There's no need at all,' Miss Perrot told her.

Bossy as usual, Priscilla thought rebelliously.

'I'm quite sure Mrs Adam has everything in that is needed for the weekend.'

Susannah Adam was a widow who lived in a cottage over the moor, with her half-witted son, and acted as caretaker for Mooncarn during the family's residence in Plynport.

'Oh, but—' Priscilla broke off at a wink and gesture unseen by Miss Perrot, from William.

'Oh, very well,' she agreed. 'Tomorrow I shall go, though. I want to see Ned.'

Ned was the sturdy nephew of Ellen and John Craze, and lived with and worked for the couple, who regretfully had no children of their own. He always had a warm welcome for the child, and a fund of stories, some amusing, some dramatic and highly coloured, of the things that had been going on in the district during her absence. Many of these were gleaned from old Tommy Treves, a pedlar, and, some said, a real 'pellar' also

44

— white witch. He travelled lanes and hamlets in that part of Cornwall selling trinkets from his donkey cart — fancy goods, and charms to ward off any illness likely to beset either human beings or cattle. He was a perky bow-legged little character, with odd eyes, one blue, one greenish brown, eccentric in dress wearing a blue smock usually with a red spotted necktie and a jaunty pointed woollen cap having a coloured feather sticking from it. He was amiable, well-known at local inns and kiddley-winks, and had a way with womenfolk and children that earned him many free meals, even an occasional bed for a night.

Susannah, the widow-woman as she was known, 'kept in' with him, because although in her practical way only a quarter of herself believed in his charms and potions, it was as well to keep on the safe side. 'You never do know,' she'd said openly more than once. 'One day he jus' *might* come bringing a healing something or other to help cure my Billy's pore brain. Miracles do happen, though tesn' likely I do admit, not where Billy's concerned.'

All the stories told by Ned Craze, Tommy Treves' 'magic', and old Susannah's absorption in cures and herb-growing, made life at Mooncarn wonderfully stimulating to Priscilla, and that Easter in the excitement of returning to the old house, not only with papa, but with Lise to show round and explain to about the ancient legends of stones and cromlechs, she temporarily forgot all about Sir Robert Tyzackass and the sorry plight of poor Lady Dorabella Starch.

During the first few days at Mooncarn she discovered that Lise could be pleasanter company than she'd thought possible at home in Plynport. For one thing she *listened*, and seemed far more competent in absorbing local legendry than the lessons she had endured drearily from Miss Perrot.

'I like it here,' Priscilla said on an afternoon when the two children had managed to escape Miss Perrot's vigilant eye for once, and taken a short ramble over the moors. It wasn't *forbidden* for them to go out alone so long as they observed certain barriers, stipulated by William, and were careful to keep to the paths, and never step on brown undergrowth entangling the great granite boulders where there could be adders.

'So do I,' conceded Lise. 'That big grey thing. *Look!* Eet has a funny face, yes? Voila! eet — how you say — *likes* me.'

Priscilla stared at a curiously carved menhir looming from tufts of heather at a lop-sided angle which suggested it might topple at any moment. One day, perhaps, if there was a minor landslide, it might. But it had been there for centuries, from pre-Druid days most probably, and superstition had it that even if it fell it would be back again in position the following day, because it possessed magic powers.

With the rays of fading sunlight streaking sideways across the distorted semblance of a macabre primitive's face, it *did* appear from a certain angle that the slits of eyes moved momentarily towards the girls. Priscilla laughed, amazed. 'It can't move. It's only stone. And anyway, why would it like *you*? Silly!'

'Just because. That's why.'

Lise lifted her dark eyes to her companion's, and there was something strangely 'knowing' and unchildlike in their gaze. With the pale hair framing her pointed small face like an aureole of white cloud lit by sun, the small child seemed suddenly 'different' to Priscilla, a being from another world — the world of legend and Celtic mystery that defied any natural explanation. Then suddenly Lise laughed. And her laughter dispelled the illusion. 'You see? I frightened you. Yes?'

'*No*. Of course you didn't. And why did you try, anyway?' She gripped Lise's hand. 'I know things about these old stones and the people who lived here once that you never will because you can't read properly, and you — you—'

'Yes?'

'You're French. This isn't *your* country — not really.'

'It is. It *is*. Papa said so. He said, "Remember you are one of us, chérie, my own little girl". Do you not believe me?'

Yes, Priscilla believed her, and because she resented Lise's use of the word 'papa', said crossly, 'Come along, it's time we went back.'

'Why?'

'Because I say so.'

'Bossy one. That's what *I* say then — a boss-cat.'

46

Priscilla could hardly believe her ears. 'Boss cat! Where did you learn that? I'm sure it wasn't from old Perrot or papa or mama.'

'Ah, no. That nice Dan. He tell me.'

'*Dan?*' Dan was the name of the boy who helped in the garden and brought vegetables in to the kitchen at Seagrave Square, sometimes assisting in the scullery on a wet day.

Lise nodded. 'Oui. He tell me funnee things often. All about her – her Ladyship, and—'

'*Mama?* Dan talks to *you* about mama?'

Lise nodded. 'I like Dan. He says I'm veree charmante, beautiful, and that when I grow up I will be the most lovelee lady in the whole world. *There.*' She lifted her head proudly. 'Tell me, Prissee, am I so? You think it? Yes?'

'I think you're absolutely awful,' Priscilla answered with a rush of anger, 'and if mama knew you've sneaked about listening to tales from Dan you'd be whipped.'

The little girl suddenly pulled away. 'No, no. You not understand. I'm not bad. Not me. Only bad people get whipped. Why not like me, Prissee?'

Priscilla's brows came together over the bridge of her nose in a frown.

'It's not that I don't like you, and not that I do,' she said. 'You're younger than me. We think differently, that's all.'

'So are we both younger than papa,' Lise commented. 'But you love heem – and me, so do I. I think age is silly.'

Priscilla did not reply. As always when Lise spoke of William as 'papa' on equal terms with herself, who'd been his real daughter for so long, she felt aggrieved and resentful. They returned to the house in silence, and Priscilla wished she'd brought her notebook with her so she could continue with the adventures of Sir Robert Tyzackass, and in doing so succeed in forgetting for the time being the troublesome presence of Lise.

William left at the end of the week, saying he'd be returning before long to enjoy more leisure and their company at Mooncarn. But Priscilla knew this was only a half-promise. Once he was away some important business or other was sure to crop up and keep him to the grindstone, as he put it.

Miss Perrot and Cook were left in charge with the children, and the man Jenkins to assist with any hard work necessary. He had also been instructed to accompany Priscilla on any riding sessions she wished. William had a young mare stabled at the farm for the purpose, and for taking Miss Perrot and her young charges to Wynk or further afield in the carriage, should they want a change.

Priscilla, however, was never bored by the surroundings of Mooncarn, and she liked nothing better than to wander about with only Mrs Jolly, her amiable dog, bouncing up and down in the undergrowth and long bracken, for company. Lise, of course, made everything different, and she didn't like dogs. 'Le chien, it bite me,' she complained one day. 'Yelp, yelp, yelp! Why does it make that so sillee noise, ha?'

'She *didn't* bite you,' Priscilla remarked sharply, 'and she never would, unless it was a mistake — a game. And when you come out with me Mrs Jolly's coming too. So there.'

Day by day, Priscilla was realising how very ignorant Lise was of so many things, animals especially. But then, of course, having lived in Paris most of her life she probably hadn't known any or ever owned a pet. On the other hand, in some ways she could be so secretive and strange. It was as though part of her had been 'grown-up' always. What was the word mama had used, Priscilla wondered one evening, as the two girls stood at the sitting room window watching the last sunlight die behind the rim of moor — 'sophisticated'. Yes that was it. Priscilla herself wasn't *completely* sure of its meaning, but she was certain it was the right one for Lise, and accurately fitted the manner she lifted her face to be kissed by papa, or looked sideways from her dark eyes at anyone she fancied from Ned the stable boy at Seagrave Square to certain of the top-hatted gentlemen friends who'd seen her by chance during her first days in the Clinton household.

Priscilla privately considered her manner was 'soppy' and did her best to ignore it. But that certain evening at Mooncarn, the familiar irritation returned, when Lise sighed and said in rather hushed tones that went oddly with her angelic exterior, 'Ah! eet is so — how you say — bee — beeootiful, yes? When night comes and the moon shines. Soon there will be a moon. When I'm a lady I will have a lover like a king. Tall, he will be, and we will make love. Do you know about love, Prissee?'

Priscilla stared. 'Love? I suppose so. I love nice things, like Mrs Jolly, papa, and riding Merlinda. Jenkins is going to take me one day, and we shall gallop right up to the Carn perhaps. I shall love that, being all free and not having to listen to Miss Perrot saying don't do this, do that, tie your hair back — all those stuffy things. I love strawberries, too,' she laughed. 'Strawberries and cream. There are so many things to love, and so many ways of loving.'

'*Non!*' Lise's response was very definite. 'There ees only *one* way of loving, I can tell you.' She nodded. 'And that ees true. Vraiment.'

Priscilla was suddenly discomforted. 'Oh, you're so stupid, Lise. *Really*. So silly. *One* way. You're limited, you really are. You ought to think more. Use your brain.'

'Ah, but I don't need to.'

'What do you mean?'

Lise didn't answer. But that night Priscilla discovered something of the truth about her half-sister.

The night was clear, lit by a pale moon climbing gradually above a thin veil of mist into the velvet dark sky. Long shadows snaked over the high moors towards the valleys and Mooncarn, patterning the wild hillside with curious zig-zagged shapes from dolmen, cromlech, and skeletal mine stack. Northwards beyond the cliffs, the sea glittered with the brilliance of black glass silvered with splashes of white where the waves broke. There was little wind, only a faint whining through heather and gorse, and the silence somehow added to the eerie atmosphere of 'place' and bygone things.

Priscilla for some unknown reason could not sleep. She wished she had a book because although Miss Perrot had taken her candle away before saying goodnight, the yellow moonlight streaming on the window was sufficiently bright to read by. As it was, she could only lie thinking about past events: the arrival of

Lise, her mother's resentment, and the unfriendly atmosphere of her parents to each other.

Between fitful periods of half dozing she visualised what boarding school might have been like, and whether her new tutor would be nice or nasty and strict, whether he'd wear glasses and look owlish as so many curates did, or if he'd be dark and handsome, with a resemblance perhaps to Sir Robert Tyzackass? If he was like Sir Robert how marvellous that would be. But then she didn't *really* think that could happen, because the only *real* one was in the book she was writing, and in her mind and heart. Oh, yes! Although she'd made him love the gipsy girl, she was secretly imagining him as her own lover, and what it would be like to have his wild stern face bent towards her, while he pressed her passionately to him, before his lips met hers. Picturing the romantic scene so vividly made her too restless just to lie there, so she sat up, went to the window and pulled the curtains wide revealing the scene outside lit to sudden magical clarity in the yellow light.

On such a night, she thought, some legendary hero of the past might have galloped down the rugged slope on his flashing black steed to rescue a fair maiden − a princesses or beautiful beggarmaid − from the clutches of the wicked villain who'd imprisoned her in a lonely castle tower. There would be a fight first, of course; a duel between the wicked lord, or perhaps not. Perhaps the hero would climb up a granite wall to a turret window, and rescue her that way. Something of the sort might easily have happened at Keigwinnen Castle which was a ruin now, not far away, beyond the ridge of the moor.

Priscilla's imagination was so alight, she didn't realise at first when she saw 'the thing' − whether it was real or not − a pale white ghostly shape, whiter than the moonlight, lifting its arms above its head, very near the lopsided ugly old menhir. Priscilla's heart raced for a second or two then missed a beat. The figure was *real*. It must be, because it lifted its shining head, and at the same moment something dark and black shadowed by thick undergrowth came out of the bushes and crawled forward. It could have been an animal, but it wasn't. After a moment it stood up and remained motionless, with an eerie greenish glow striking on the round disc-like countenance.

A *man*.

And the man was small — with a leap of apprehension Priscilla *knew*, recognised even from that distance the grotesque ape-like form and blank staring countenance of old Susannah's son, Abel. That wasn't all. The white shape turned towards him, pale hair caught on a frail shiver of rising wind, and there they stood, like creatures of the elements beneath the ancient menhir, as though on some secret tryst. 'Lise,' thought Priscilla, with a mixture of wild emotions rising in her. '*Lise!* and she's got *nothing on*.'

She felt excited and horrified at the same time; horrified because although *she'd* longed often to be able to race across the moors and bathe in the streams without the constriction of clothes, Lise's feelings were quite different. Lise wasn't the same as other people; she was like Abel in one way, though not so bad — *brainless* however lovely, and because of her beauty, dangerous.

Hurriedly and as quietly as possible, Priscilla pulled on a pair of soft-soled shoes, slipped into her woolly dressing gown, very carefully opened her door, and went out. She tip-toed along the landing, passing Lise's bedroom door and Miss Perrot's next to it, pausing every few seconds to hear if anyone had been disturbed. There was no sound, nothing but that of the old clock ticking on the landing. Everyone, luckily, must be asleep. It was already after one o'clock and it was hardly likely the governess would be awake. Miss Perrot took her 'little doses' of something promptly at ten to ensure, she said, that she had a night's proper rest. All the same, Priscilla took no chances, and when at last she reached a side door of the house leading almost straight to the moor, she pulled the bolt slowly and softly so that it made no squeak. Then she slipped out, and on light quick feet made her way up the thread of path upwards towards the menhir.

All the time, pushing brambles and gorse aside as her pace increased, she tried to believe she was mistaken, that when she reached the old menhir there'd be no Lise — she'd somehow

51

mistaken a spreading patch of flowering thorn washed white by the moon for the little girl, and that only Abel would be there. Perhaps he'd have gone too, she hoped so. She wasn't *afraid* of him. At least, she tried not to be. It was just the vacant way he had of staring and saying nothing that discomforted her. Once, he'd followed her when she'd gone out alone, and she'd stopped and said, 'Hullo, Abel,' because she'd sensed intuitively it was wiser to be friendly — if he liked her he couldn't turn nasty. Abel had never been known to hurt anyone or anything, but there was something about him that made her *unsure*, although she didn't know what of.

With her heart bumping against her ribs because she'd been running for the last part of the way, she rounded two large boulders and ahead of her saw them. What she'd imagined was *true*.

Abel! with his long arms hanging limply by his sides, staring at the delicate white form confronting him from small eyes, mouth agape, unmoving as the granite stones scattering the moor. And Lise was smiling; her smile was so innocent and lovely, and yet so wise with developing primitive knowledge that Priscilla was shaken, disturbed. No shred of clothing hid an inch of her white skin. She was completely naked, and also motionless, except for the movement of one hand gently stroking a virgin small breast. Her cape lay on the ground by her tiny feet. On the breeze her white-gold hair floated gently behind her shoulders like a bridal veil of some wild elfin creature longing for — what?

For seconds Priscilla was dumb. Then she rushed forward and caught the child by a shoulder. 'Lise, what are you doing here? And like that?' She reached for the cape and flung it round the small figure. At the same moment, Abel turned and plunged clumsily past a group of twisted alders, disappearing into the shadows of heather and furze darkening the shape of hill.

Without realising it, Priscilla was shaking her sister. 'Don't you *see* — he's not — Abel's funny; he's not *right*, and for you to undress like that! Don't you *understand*? What would old Perrot think? And papa? *Lise*, what's the matter with you?'

Lise turned her brilliant eyes on her sister for a moment, then suddenly they filled with tears.

'Why you so cross? I not bad. Not me, not me. It was the light, and those – those—' she gulped.

'Yes?'

'Those *things* dancing. I thought – me, Lise, *I* can dance too—'

'What do you mean *things*?' Shadows?'

Lise nodded vigorously.

'Mais oui. Yes, shadows. And you can't dance, not properly, not with capes on and things. Don't you *see*, Prissee? Oh, Prissee, please be nice. Love me a bit, just a leetle bit, Prissee. You won't tell papa, will you? Or – or Mademoiselle?'

Priscilla knew suddenly she wouldn't, because part of her understood.

'No. It's all right. I won't tell. Only come along now. There'd be an awful fuss if we were discovered. But if you do it again I shall. And you'll be beaten. So you'd better keep your promise.'

'I will, I really *will*, Prissee. But, oh, eet was nice out there. At first eet was so – how you say – exciting, before—'

'Shut up! Be quiet,' Priscilla commanded quite roughly, using a harshness and manner of speech that would have been seriously condemned by Miss Perrot. Lise lowered her head and started to cry, unhappy gulping sobs like those of any baby.

'Oh for goodness sake – don't be so *soft*. And keep your cape closed. If anyone saw us from a window there'd be an *awful* fuss. You should be thankful *I* saw you and no one else, except Abel of course.'

The name caught Lise's attention immediately, and she stopped crying. 'Ees that what he's called – A b e l?' She spoke each letter carefully as though trying to imprint it on her mind.

'Yes. And you'd better not mention it to anyone, not *any*one. And keep out of his way. He's a—'

'A what, Prissee?'

'A half-wit.'

'A half-weet? What's that?'

'Oh—' Exasperated, Priscilla gripped her sister's shoulder

53

and jerked her ahead at a sharper pace. 'Not all there,' she retorted, '*lacking* — like you. Now hurry, don't ask such stupid questions.'

Half running down the incline between the flickering shadows of the moor, the children soon reached the house. Priscilla pushed the side door furtively. It was all right, no-one was about.

When Lise was safely in the small bedroom allotted to her, Priscilla went to her own. She took off her boots and wrap and drew the window curtains close. Her heart was still beating quickly and it was some time after getting into bed before she slept.

When at last she did it was to dream not of the amazing history of Sir Robert Tyzackass, but of Lise grown up, a mad young queen in a white robe, with her pale hair flying. Round her were kneeling lumpy figures like huge grey stones, and all had the same kind of face resembling the gaping countenance of Abel Adam. Voices were moaning and there was a shrieking wind. At that point, Priscilla woke up with a start, to find the wind was real and the moaning sound came from the creaking of the window. She lay still, until the thumping of her heart eased. Then she got up and pulled the curtains open. The morning was grey, with a cold clear light over the blue of hills and sea. Sounds of movement came from below, of Cook and the girl stirring, and the firm tread of men's boots, followed by the thumping noise of a bucket being dumped, containing logs probably for the fires.

Lise was very quiet at breakfast. How much she recollected of the night's events Priscilla didn't know. Miss Perrot stared at the child critically and said, 'You look a little pale, Lise, my dear. Do you feel quite well?'

Lise nodded and gave an angelic smile. 'Mais oui, mam'selle. I mean, *thank* you. Yes, veree well.'

The smile of satisfaction on Miss Perrot's face died as she turned to Priscilla. 'And you? You're not eating much. Come now. Finish your porridge.'

Looking faintly hostile, Priscilla said, 'I don't *feel* like it.'

'Priscilla!' The cold voice held a warning note.

'Well, I don't.'

'Oh! very well. Perhaps you're a little out of sorts. We must all three take a brisk walk on the moors this morning. You *did* have rather a lot of cream yesterday. You may be liverish.'

Priscilla sighed. Then, doing the best to be polite, because the last thing she wanted just then was to have a scene with 'old Perrot', she remarked, 'I don't think it's my liver, Miss Perrot, and if you don't mind I'd rather take Mrs Jolly through the fields. She loves the grass, and — and I've things to think about.'

Miss Perrot's eyebrows shot up in amazement. '*Really!* May I enquire what kind of things, Priscilla.'

Priscilla lowered her long lashes, looking evasively downwards.

'Do you mind! I'd rather not say just yet. It's something — about books and things. One day, perhaps—' she broke off hesitantly.

A small, slightly condescending smile twitched the governess's lips. 'Ah! so you have a secret. Very well, my dear. We must all be allowed our little — idiosyncrasies, I suppose. And we must remember that your dog must be kept carefully on the leash in case she worries the sheep.'

'*We!*' Priscilla thought, meaning that Perrot meant to join her with Lise. Well, she wouldn't have a chance, because at the first opportunity she'd have sneaked out the back way with Mrs Jolly and they'd be off on their own. It was so lovely now, with the valley fields smelling of young green grass, and already starred with the small white daisies and a few early buttercups. As for sheep! There weren't any except for the small black-faced hill kind on the moors, and anyway Mrs Jolly had been taught when she was a puppy not to chase them.

Oh, it was so good to be alone, she thought, a little later, as she made her way in the opposite direction of Trencrowse, towards sloping grasslands and the small patchworked area of fields bordered either by stone walls, or hedgerows already alight with patches of foaming wild blossom. Without anyone to disturb her with stupid remarks she could 'think' properly about her developing novel, at the same time enjoying her zest for physical excitement and exercise. Sometimes she leaped for joy, then ran ahead, with Mrs Jolly yelping at her heels, and the whole world seemed to be singing. Life was going to be so *wonderful*. So much lay ahead! So much to savour and learn, and love. Just for the moment, though, imagining it was all enough, with the sweet spring wind brushing her face and all the sounds and scents of early morning whipping her senses to an overwhelming delight.

Of course, when she got back Miss Perrot was waiting for her. 'Where *have* you been, miss?' she enquired coldly. 'All this time out on your own, and I thought it was arranged for Lise and myself to accompany you. I waited and waited. Then when Cook told me you'd taken that dog out, I took just a short stroll with Lise. *Really!* It was most *unkind* of you. And look at you, your hair's all loose and briars on your gown.'

'Where?'

'*There!*' replied the governess, pointing to a small leaf and twig caught near the hem of Priscilla's dress.

Priscilla stooped and plucked it out. 'The blossom was out,' she said, changing the subject. 'And there were primroses. Lots.'

'I didn't ask about primroses. I would just like to know if you spoke to anyone. Was Abel around? Or anyone else?'

After a wicked sidelong look at Lise, Priscilla said casually, with assumed innocence, 'Only Sir Robert Tyzackass.'

For a moment Miss Perrot was speechless. Then she exclaimed, 'Sir Robert *Tyzackass*? Now who is *he*, may I ask? I've never heard of anyone round here with such an *extraordinary* name. And I'm sure it can't be real. Whowever he was he must have been spinning some stupid tale to you − a gipsy perhaps. Was that it? Some lowborn tinker trying to wheedle family secrets out of you, how many doors there are at the back of Mooncarn, or some such knowledge, so that the house could be plundered some night. Tell me, Priscilla, at once. What was he like? − A play actor, perhaps? I've heard there's a fair on at Wynk next week, and actors are very sly people. Rogues, mostly.'

Laughter bubbled in Priscilla's throat, but she managed to restrain it.

'Oh, no, Miss Perrot. He wasn't an actor or a gipsy. He was dark and handsome, and *very* gallant. He doffed his hat to me and asked my name, then he told me his, and said good day to me, and rode on.'

'Was he on a horse then?'

'Yes. A shining black one.' Her description, at that point, really *did* appear to impress Miss Perrot. So much so that Priscilla felt mildly guilty. But then she hadn't *really* been fibbing, had she? Sir Robert Tyzackass *was* real to her, and had been with her all the time. Anyway, if it gave poor old Perrot a thrill she'd done a good deed — in a way.

'I shall have to make enquiries about this,' she heard the governess saying meditatively. 'Ty — what did you say the name was?'

'Tyzackass.'

'I shall call in at the post office when next I go to Wynk, and find out if there really is a titled family of such a strange name in the district.'

'He may have galloped for miles,' Priscilla retorted. 'He didn't say where his home was. But I expect it's some stately mansion somewhere.'

'I can always enquire from Debrett,' said Miss Perrot. 'They'll know. If the man was an impostor his name won't be recorded.'

The subject was dropped there, and in spite of the governess's firm intention to make local enquiries before going any further with the matter, the mysterious Sir Robert Tyzackass was completely forgotten two days later, when news was brought to Mooncarn from William that the family were to return immediately, as Lady Elizabeth had had a serious heart attack, from which it was feared she could not recover.

Bags and belongings were hastily packed, with everyone at Mooncarn in a state of shock except Lise, who appeared completely calm and mostly unaware of what was happening.

When they arrived at Seagrave Square it was to find all the blinds of Number 7 carefully closed across the windows. The evening was grey, and Priscilla felt a shudder of fear shiver her spine.

Lady Elizabeth Clinton had died that afternoon.

3

For weeks after Elizabeth's death William was uncharacteristi-
cally withdrawn, grieving silently not so much for the loss of a
wife and partner – it had been a considerable time since she had
fitted either role – but over the knowledge that they had both so
mutually failed each other, she through her complete lack of
warmth and affection, he in his incapacity to fathom her excessive sensibilities and demands at all times for the genteel facade
due to her own social status. To try to deceive himself that he
missed her *personally*, would have been an anachronism, and
quite untrue. And as time passed he realised that a load of
responsibility had been taken from his shoulders. Even as
hostess at his table she had seldom appeared during the last few
months, and it was well known to the servants and doubtless
beyond, that William Clinton and his lady wife had become an
ill-matched pair.

They always had been, he told himself frequently with glum
honesty. He should have had the good sense to have chosen a
sturdier more compatible woman for his marriage bed, one
from a humbler background with an understanding of the
needs of a man of his type. In wedding her he had done her a
disservice, although at the time her family had benefited more
than anyone guessed. Still, it was over now. He had work, and
Priscilla, child of his heart, that intelligent wayward tomboy of
a girl possessing attributes of both parents, and a few of the fail-
ings, too.

As for Lise! well, she was a beauty, whatever else might be
said of her. And that 'whatever else' he was prepared to shrug
off for a time, because its possibilities mildly troubled him.

Priscilla was genuinely upset by her mother's death. In her

life, though, they'd never been close; Elizabeth had been something mysterious and beautiful in the background, a frail wilt-
ing lily figure like the Lady of Shalott, but with a surprising
capacity to lay down the law at intervals, which had kept the
household in awe.

Now she was gone.

However, the loss was not so depressing as it might have been,
due to the arrival of the new tutor whose presence helped dispel
to a certain extent the morbid shadow of the recent gloomy
events.

He was a slight pale young man, not at all 'owlish-looking' as
Priscilla had anticipated, but fair-haired, with good features
and keen blue eyes. His chin, perhaps, was a little weak, but was
belied by the mouth which could be surprisingly firm when he
was serious. Priscilla decided that she would probably find him
pleasant to get along with, but was inwardly disappointed he
could not have borne a slight resemblance to Sir Robert
Tyzackuss. There was nothing faintly exciting about him. Still,
anything was better than old Perrot. So she decided not to be
troublesome, but to try her hardest — at first, anyway — to
please him. He was clever, Papa said, even brilliant, and she
wanted to learn all she could, especially about literature and
languages, since she was determined to be a famous writer when
she was grown up.

When her mama had been alive the stipulation had been that
if boarding school was shelved, she would still have to endure a
year at finishing school, either in Switzerland or France, before
she was 'brought out'. But with mama not on the scene to be forever badgering papa about this, in Priscilla's opinion 'silly' business, she could probably wheedle her father into forgetting it or
perhaps into allowing her to have a period at university. Women
weren't supposed to go to university but she didn't see why they
shouldn't, and such a course was surely much more creditable to
any girl with ambitions than spending weary hours embroidering
or painting little watercolours, and learning to play the piano
and recite and sing sentimental ballads in stuffy drawing-rooms.

Privately, William agreed with Priscilla, up to a point, but wanting the very best in life for his daughter both socially, and mentally, he recognised that despite the hypocrisy of current society the recognition of certain rules could be helpful later to her in achieving a suitable marriage. A niggling sense of conscience told him also that he probably owed this observance to the wishes of his dead wife.

However, for the moment he shelved the problem, and to help allay a morbid awareness of time's passing, devoted himself with increased purpose to his work. The girls, for the time being, seemed all right; Lise, cared for by the devoted and ever watchful Maud Perrot, was an entrancing well-behaved little thing to have about, although he was frequently embarrassed by her passionate show of affection for himself. Priscilla appeared to have got over the loss of her mother extremely well, and had impressed her tutor by her bright mind and developing knowledge of the classics. Indeed, she had already proved herself clever beyond her years, and seldom now made spelling mistakes in her written compositions in English which covered a variety of subjects. Occasionally, unpredictably, she'd decided she was sick of lessons for the day, and told him so.

'I want to go out,' she'd say, or words to that effect. 'Thoughts won't come when I'm stuck in all day.' She did not add that she wanted to be alone in the daffodil wood which was reached through a side door from the walled-in garden of number 3, at the back of the house, or that unless she could skip and run and feel the fresh air on her face, she'd go all sad inside and remember mama.

Oh yes; whatever anyone else might think, including papa, there were moments when sadness swept over her in a wave of loneliness because she had never been able to be close with Elizabeth or to make her happy. Mrs Jolly was her only comfort at such times. Mrs Jolly and the strange longing inside her that whispered, 'You are *you*, Priscilla Clinton. The world is a lovely place and everything is waiting for you. It's all there – the life that makes the trees and flowers grow, and the apple blossom against the blue sky. One day something *wonderful* is going to happen to you, something that belongs to everyone, but is yours alone, in a different way.' Such confusion of emotion of course could not properly be expressed in words, but the young man, her tutor seemed to understand, and never argued with her when that certain light filled her limpid eyes of joy mingled with sadness, and deep inner hunger for experience.

'Very well,' he'd say usually. 'Off with you on your secret jaunt. We'll make up with an extra bit of history tomorrow.'

So time passed. Life at Seagrave Square gradually settled down into its new routine. Everything educationally and domestically assumed a normal and apparently satisfactory pattern, although William was forced to recognise that Lise might prove to be an unexpected problem as she grew older.

There was one occasion when she appeared suddenly in the library wearing one of her mother's gowns with the skirt drawn back and pinned in the form of a bustle. The gown was of diaphanous, palest blue, cut so low in front as to be half falling off the shoulders. She had grown considerably during the past two years, and with her hair caught up on top of the head gave the impression momentarily of young developing womanhood. William was alone, having dismissed his secretary for the day, half an hour before. Hearing the door open he straightened his back, jerked the chair, and stared. It was early evening, and the slanting beams of the oil lamp on the table gave a sensuous mystery to the lines of figure — immature breasts and thighs, revealing that she was wearing nothing beneath.

After the first shock, anger stirred in him. Where the hell was Perrot? And what the devil was she thinking about to allow this girl, this, this *child* of his — for dammit she *was* a child — to bedeck herself like any wanton seductress in his wife's clothes? Yes! his dead wife's — Elizabeth's.

'What are you doing here, looking like that?' he demanded harshly. 'Go upstairs at once and dress decently.' He paused before adding, 'And tell Miss Perrot I wish to see her at once.'

Her eyelashes fluttered, her head drooped. Then she lifted her quivering face and ran towards him, arms extended, looking more poignantly lovely in her distress than any girl — or woman, for that matter — had a right to.

'But papa!' Already the tears were flooding her eyes. 'I *love* you papa. I want you to *like* me — yes? And so I, I took eet from her — from Mama's closet — and eet was so lovely.' A youthful pale hand stroked the gauzy material above the gently developing curves. 'Do you not think so, papa?' She stood on tiptoe, reaching for his shoulders. He could not help being aware of a drift of perfume, and soft pearly sheen of her skin where the blue material slipped. Revolted by the stirring of male instinct and desire long since controlled and quelled, he pushed her away.

'Behave yourself. Do you realise what you're doing? Little girls like you should be — should be—'

'Whipped, papa? But I would not mind being beaten by you. Not eef I am so bad.'

Clenching both hands, with the hot blood rushing to his face, he said thickly, 'Leave this room *immediately*. And never let me see you like that again. Do you understand? Or you'll be sent away. You shall be placed in the Convent of Saint Maria where the strict nuns will see to it that you learn right from wrong.'

'Oh no. Oh *no*.' Her voice was a wail. 'I — I only wished to *please* you, papa.'

He turned away, and stood rigidly with his hands behind his back, staring into the fire, waiting for her to go. When there was no sound he swung round again, and something in his face frightened her.

'Did you *hear me*?'

'Oui! yes, yes.' She rushed to the door, caught a toe in the fine lacy hem of the gown and fell. He didn't go to her assistance, but watched her get up, and seeing she was all right he forced himself to move, picked up a rug lying over the chesterfield, and taking three strides, flung it at her feet.

'Put that on. And keep it there until you reach your room. And if anything like this happens again, to my knowledge, you know what will happen.'

'The nuns?'

'Yes, the nuns.'

After this episode, William realised that something very

important indeed was missing from his life. He needed a wife, and the girls needed someone to take the place of a mother. Business and work, however creative, were not sufficient for a healthy home existence. So from that moment he started looking.

*

Olivia Wymberley-Brown was a widow of two years, whose husband's estate when he died, had proved far smaller than was generally believed, and his debts considerably higher. Though nonplussed and bitterly disappointed, Olivia nevertheless had made the most of what was left, and during the brief period following his demise had managed to assume a 'gallant front', as the saying went, and a ravishing exterior by spending the comparative pittance left in cultivating the smart set, and enhancing the good looks she'd been born with.

William was quite aware of the sorry state of her bank balance, and that didn't worry him in the least. That she desperately needed security with, if possible, the social status of marriage to a man such as himself, was also quite clear to him. Neither had the least illusion about the other. Sexually, commonsense told him, she would be an adequate and willing partner. She was witty, amusing, with a certain dash and coquetry about her that appealed to his ironic sense. About her origins she was evasive, but at least told no lies. So all things considered, he decided to take the plunge, proposed, and was accepted.

They were married in the early autumn of 1854, shortly before Britain's disastrous defeat at Balaclava by the Russians in the Crimean War.

The ceremony was a quiet one held at Plynport Register Office. Priscilla, then fourteen years old, and Lise twelve, were 'attendants', although the elder child had at first objected. 'I don't know, papa,' she'd said, when told the news by William. 'She won't be my *own* mama, will she? And she won't be wearing a white dress and veil. Why has *any*one got to be an attendant?'

'Because I want us to be a *family*, my dear,' William had replied firmly. 'And you want to please me, don't you?'

'Yes, of course. But—'

'Well then, that's settled,' her father had said cheerfully, rubbing his hands together as though dispelling any niggling argument about the forthcoming ceremony.

There had been no such doubt on Lise's part. 'Lovely,' she'd exclaimed, smiling radiantly. 'What shall we wear, papa?'

'Now *that*, I think, is a matter for Miss Perrot, and perhaps Olivia — your future mama.'

With a stubborn underlip outthrust, Priscilla had suggested, 'Why don't you let Lise be just the *one* attendant? What suits her would look stupid on me. She likes pinks and blues and frilly clothes. And anyway, I don't *really* like dressing up. There'll be photographers there I suppose, and — oh—' She'd broken off, longing to say, 'Why have you got to get married at all? If it's a *hostess* you want, someone to sit at the end of the table like mama used to do, I shall soon be old enough—' but of course such a remark would have been stupid. Papa didn't only want a hostess. He wanted the other things, the things that happened in bed, between a man and a woman, secret intimacies of which she'd managed to glean a certain information during the past two years.

So she'd resigned herself to the inevitable, and as a concession Priscilla had been allowed, on Olivia's instigation, to choose the colour of the gowns, a soft shade of deep hyacinth, which although it did nothing to enhance Lise's radiant enchanting looks certainly brought out the subtle lights of Priscilla's clear eyes, the stable tones of her shining hair, and soft glow of her cream skin delicately flushed at her high cheek bones.

'You know that girl of yours is going to be a beauty later on,' Olivia had said after the ceremony to William. 'Elusive, nothing blatant. But remote, and with a will of her own. I hope she comes to like me.'

'And Lise?'

'Ah well!' Olivia had shrugged and thrown him a wry almost cynical glance. 'She's a charmer, of course. Very — French.'

'Now what do you mean by that?'

'You know quite well, I'm sure. It's written all over her. No

64

brains at all, but enough allure to ensnare a Duke, or land her in the gutter. She could end up anywhere.'

William had laughed, but his expression had been briefly worried. After a pause he'd said, 'A charmer describes her exactly, but she isn't so brainless as you seem to think. That prim governess has worked wonders with the child during the last year or two.'

'Have you ever considered sending her away to school?'

'No. She couldn't cope.'

'I suppose not. And Priscilla?'

'Priscilla's education is doing very well under young John Lord. He's quite amazed at her academic prowess, especially the classics and English. He even suggested, very tentatively, that she should go on to study further, although I think Prissy had put it into his head. I squashed that immediately.'

'*Why?*'

The abrupt question startled him. 'Dammit, Livia, you should know. Girls, especially in *her* position, aren't bred to be old maids and blue-stockings. I've got far pleasanter plans ahead for my Priscilla.'

'Marriage, I suppose. To some rich businessman.'

He flung her a wry glance.

'Happiness first, Livvy.'

'My dear—' Her tone was light, playful. 'Why not both? Young love without a penny can be entrancing, I grant you. But the rich businessman can go a long way, ensuring it endures.'

With his warm glance appraisingly on the luscious lines of her elegant, though slightly plump, figure – she was, after all, past forty – he said with faint irony, an irony mingled with an unexpected wave of jealousy concerning her past the past of which she seldom spoke, '—as you have found.'

'Yes, dear, as I have found.'

'You have no illusion, have you?'

'No.' She smiled brilliantly, the long diamond ear-rings quivering beneath the satin shine of her black hair.

'In other words, if I'd been a struggling poor man you'd not have looked at me twice?'

She laughed; it was a throaty sound — seductive.

'Darling, I'd certainly have looked. You're quite a man, you know — those flashing eyes, and marvellous black sideburns. Oh, yes, I'd have fallen for you with my senses, but I'm afraid with my two legs I'd have walked away.'

'Good God! you've a nerve.'

'Of course. But you knew that, didn't you? I was always honest with you. Now you can't deny it.'

'No,' he agreed grudgingly.

'And you were careful to avoid any embarrassing probing.'

He realised what she said was true. He'd known it, of course, but her admission put so — blatantly, irritated him, and irritation gradually burned and accelerated into overwhelming sexual desire. So far, in the short time of their marriage, he'd been courteous and considerate with her. Now suddenly he faced reality — she was his. He'd bought her. She'd be generous enough to oblige in anything reasonable he asked of her. But her 'giving' would be far less than his. She would never be able to share his ambitions, or rather the dreams that inspired them. Had he been short-sighted? A fool, in taking so worldly a creature as wife?

No, dammit. Just reckless, physically, as was his wont. And he'd see he got his fair share and a bit over, in that quarter.

They were standing in the dining room during that brief conversation. He strode quickly to the main entrance leading into the hall, locked it, and returned to confront her with something hot, demanding and lascivious in his eyes which she'd never seen before.

'Come here,' he said without preamble, lifting a finger up beckoningly. Her mouth opened slightly. She stared, as her brows arched over her long cat-like eyes. When she didn't move he made one long stride forwards, encircled her waist with an arm, then, with the other, loosened the silk material low over her shoulder and pearl-cream breast, letting his hot passionate lips travel the soft skin.

She gave a short laugh, and made a feeble attempt to move

away. He swept her up, and carried her into the conservatory's steamy interior of rare and exotic plants.

'William,' she managed to say protestingly. 'Not here—'

'Here and now, my love.'

'But the servants—'

'The servants have no access, and the gardeners are both away for the afternoon. Don't worry. The luscious orchids have no tongues to talk with.'

Amazement, combined with a certain amused apprehension, revealed itself in her astonished gaze. She didn't resist, although she decided later that the whole incident had been somewhat naive and lacking in good taste for two individuals of their sophistication and maturity. At the moment, however, having no choice in the matter, she succumbed to his ravishing with only a faint show of resistance that inflamed his ardour more. His hands were first gentle, then hard on her satin-smooth flesh. In spite of herself she eventually found her senses roused, though her head remained cool. At the peak of culmination, despite her body's reaction of instinctive response, her attention was purposefully involved elsewhere, in the heady sultry sweetness of the air, the pattern of trailing leaves above their heads, and the knowledge that it would soon be over — this ridiculous show of two human bodies heaving convulsively on a well-cushioned piece of garden furniture. Such antics could be bearable, even enjoyable, in the bedroom. But *there*! 'Well, really, William,' she thought as he at last finished his gyrations and released her, buttoning his clothes a trifle self-consciously, 'I didn't expect it.'

Perhaps she should have done, but it would have made no difference. His roots were those of a peasant, unique of the breed, but fundamentally true to type. And she? A secret glow of satisfaction filled her. She was no better, just a little cleverer perhaps, because the price she'd paid in their mutual bargain had been meagre, compared to what she'd received in return.

She just wished awakening hadn't been forced upon her quite so soon. A little romance would have been pleasurable, and perhaps even induced a faint illusion of love.

But somehow this conservatory affair had effectively dispelled any such possibility. So she would accept her lot, and bask in the full glory and achievement of being Mrs William Clinton. All she wanted materially she'd damn well have, and to hell with dreams.

*

Meanwhile, at the precise time of papa's connubial incident with Priscilla's new 'mama', Priscilla was secluded in the gazebo working on the theme of a new, and in her own opinion, far more adult novel. *Passionate Love*, or *The Adventures of Sir Robert Tyzackass* had been sent, during the past two years to three publishers under the nom-de-plume of Cornelia Almond, which she'd thought sounded unusual and adult. Only Cook had been in her confidence and had posted the manuscript, with a letter and stamps asking for it to be returned if unsuitable to Poste Restante, Plynport main office. Two of the publishers had quickly turned down the manuscript with the usual letter of rejection. The third however, had been more personal, and advised the authoress to make the story perhaps a little less melodramatic, or to use a more practical theme dealing in matters more concerned with real life.'

My dear Miss Almond,

Having read your book I am afraid we cannot make an offer to publish it. However, as a writer you have many points to commend you, a vivid imagination and descriptive ability which gives considerable promise for the future. I am taking the liberty of assuming you are young? Therefore, I hope very much you will not let refusal of *Passionate Love* deter you from trying again. It is obvious you have talent, and with a little more experience and practical approach may make a name one day in the writing world.

We shall be interested to read further works of yours when you have any to offer.

A word of advice — watch your spelling.

Yours with all good wishes.

Edward Blakey.

'Well!' Cook had said, having read the letter. 'I'm sure he's a very nice gentleman, that Mister Blakey. 'Make your name in the writing world' — that's a *real* compliment. Mark my words, Miss Priscilla, he's got faith in you, or he'd never bother to write like that. These clever men can generally spot genius when it's there.'

'Do you *think* so, Mrs James — *really*?' Priscilla asked, with a rush of colour to her face.

'Of course I do,' Cook said, using the rolling pin vigorously on her flat slab of pastry. 'Now don't you be too disappointed. Don't give up. Many writers would give their eyes for a letter like that. All you've got to do now is think of another character with an easier name perhaps — Smith? — or Brown?'

'Oh *no*. They're so ordinary, so *stuffy*.'

'Well then, there's Paynter, or Pengelly, both true Cornish names, or Phillips. What about Phillips?'

'I'll have to think,' Priscilla had answered. 'I thought Tyzackass was so *good*. Colourful. I made it up myself.'

'Oh yes, but then most folks like names they know, names maybe they have themselves. I may be wrong o' course. But when I settle to a good book, I do tend to imagine myself as the chief character — what *I'd* do in his place, or hers. Another thing—'

'Yes?'

'Gipsies aren't all that popular. You can have them in the background, I s'pose. But not as the heroine.'

Priscilla didn't see why not. In her opinion, a beautiful Romany girl with flying black tresses who could dance the Flamenco in twirling skirts, all wild and free, was far more attractive than a lady-like creature such as Lady Dorabella Starch. However, she thought over what Mrs James had said, and had come to the conclusion that she might be right. What a bore! Of course, *Jane Eyre* by Currer Bell published only a year or two ago, had an ordinary-looking heroine who wasn't really at all ordinary herself, and what a success that story was. Priscilla sighed. Actually, *she* didn't like anything ordinary, and she wasn't sure that Mr Rochester really would have fallen in love with the rather severe-looking little Jane.

Thinking of Mr Rochester brought Sir Robert Tyzackass vividly to mind again. If only she could meet someone like him, she was sure there'd be instant attraction between them, providing she was careful to appear at her very best, and was wearing her most attractive and colourful gown to emphasise her youthful developing figure and glossy sheen of her soft sable hair which on rare special occasions she was allowed to have arranged in an adult manner.

Olivia encouraged vanity in her stepdaughter. Being herself extremely vain and spending William's money like water, after the period of enforced restraint following her late husband's death, she felt justified that Priscilla also should share the delights of being rich. Miss Perrot strongly disapproved, and even had a word in her employer's ear about his offspring's extravagant inclinations. William, in his turn, spoke of it to his wife. She shrugged her fine shoulders effectively, and with a note of derisive pity in her voice said:

'Poor plain creature. You know, William, that woman is the perfect specimen of frustrated femininity. Priscilla's growing up now. You surely wish her to make the best of herself?'

'Naturally. But—'

'There can really be no buts about her clothes, dear. And good dressing costs money. Do you grudge it her? If it were Lise it would be a different matter. Lise will get by, make an impression, in anything. But Prissy needs her best points emphasising.' There was a pause then she added emphatically, 'Of course, it's up to you.'

Day by day, William was discovering that more than he'd anticipated was up to him. Olivia's lavish spending in giving expensive dinner parties, taking expensive jaunts to London and Paris, ordering jewellery and clothes willy-nilly without consulting him, changing and employing extra staff and in every way increasing the expensive manner of their life style was making a considerable hole in even *his* pocket.

He remonstrated on occasion, but refused to make a quarrel of the issue, telling himself that in time, when Olivia had grown accustomed to the novelty of excessive spending, she would become bored and no longer have any passion for it. This, how-ever, did not prove to be the case, and eventually, when she suggested taking a trip to the Americas in the autumn of that year, he put his foot down.

'No, I'm afraid not, my dear. I shan't have long enough at that period to make much of a break, and it would cost a very great deal to do it in your style—'

'Cost?' she broke in uncomprehendingly. 'Whenever did the wealthy William Clinton have to think of *cost*?'

'You see him standing before you now. I've tried to give you all you've wanted so far, Olivia. But America, at the moment, is definitely *off*. I've other commitments, and certain things on my mind which demand my attention. This summer, and for as long as you like, Mooncarn's at your disposal.'

Any trace of a disbelieving smile that had been on her face vanished. After a perceptive pause in which she did not attempt to hide her annoyance, she said coldly, 'I see.'

'I hope you do,' he returned stiffly. 'The fact is that if certain possibilities arise in – in business affairs, we may have to draw in our horns a little.'

'*What* business affairs? Or mayn't I be allowed to ask?'

'Certainly you may ask. *The Fair Maiden* built to my design, in which I personally also invested quite heavily, unfortunately went aground due to faulty navigation. How long it will be before she is salvaged and got afloat again I don't know. I have also gone bond for a friend of mine in whose integrity I had the greatest faith and still have. It concerns a certain construction scheme up country, which appears to be running into trouble. It's possible I may have to fork out a little fortune if called upon.'

'But *you* of all men must have been sure of what you were doing.'

'I was, and I still feel I was right. Unfortunately, one can never be a hundred per cent certain about some completely fresh interference of nature. In this case – water.'

'Well, it seems incomprehensible to me—' She shrugged, gave a dry little sound meant presumably to be a laugh, but certainly wasn't.

'Still,' she added offhandedly, 'I'm no business woman.'

'Aren't you? Not in my way, perhaps. In your own though I'd say you'd considerable ability.'

Her eyes narrowed. They stared at each other momentarily like two primitive creatures assessing mutual potentialities, then, with a shrug, she turned away and proceeded to arrange flowers on the table.

And so that year, at the beginning of August, the family once again set off for Mooncarn.

And it was there, for the first time, that Priscilla set eyes on Jason Blakey.

He was tall, bronzed, fair-haired, with eyes of the most startling blue she'd ever seen, a young man of twenty-five with the unmistakable look about him of a seafarer, although he'd fought in the Crimea, and survived even the ill-managed and tragic episode of Balaclava, in which he'd been wounded and released from further service. He was repainting the stern of a small yacht when Priscilla, wandering about the cove on her own, chanced to notice him, and instantly felt a thrill of something new and exciting stir her veins. Her blue frock was held hunched up in front, almost to her knees, and a pair of stockings fell over one arm. Her feet were bare, glistening from sand and sunshine; every second or two she kicked the soft shingle with her toes, and shook her long sable-tawny hair back over her shoulders so the warm sea-blown wind brushed her glowing skin with sensuous impact. He glanced up as she approached and smiled.

'Hullo,' he said.

'Hullo,' her reply was hesitant, almost a whisper.

He bent down again with his brush, then after a short dab here and there, jumped to his feet. He was not quite so tall as she'd thought, a little under six feet probably, muscular and athletic-looking, with a scar running down one brown arm. She could imagine him having strange adventures in faraway lands, guessed instinctively, that he must have travelled and would never be content with an ordinary everyday kind of life. He wasn't handsome exactly, not in the conventional way — his strong nose had a chunky end, and his smile was a bit lopsided. His eyebrows slanted upwards, and his fair hair sprang up rebelliously from a wide forehead, the sort of hair that would refuse to lie down or be groomed to any pattern. But these idiosyncrasies, only added to his attraction, in Priscilla's opinion. Oh, he was like nobody she'd ever seen before. She was at once confused, exhilarated, and astonished at the tide of feeling sweeping her. And when he said, 'We haven't met before, have we?' she had difficulty in answering coherently. 'No – no. I'm – I'm Priscilla – Priscilla Clinton.'

'*Clinton!*' He smiled properly then. 'You mean William's daughter? Of Mooncarn?'

'Yes.'

'Well, I'll be damned,' he extended his right hand. 'Pleased to greet you, Miss Clinton. I'm Jason Blakey, of the Blakey Shipping Line, acquaintance, and I hope friend, of your father.'

A rush of joy intermingled with embarrassment at being addressed in such an adult way by this exciting stranger, brought a wave of rose red to her already sunburned cheeks.

'Just fancy!' she said. 'How funny—'

His brows shot up. 'Funny? Glad you find me amusing.' Then he grinned as the sunlight caught the fine lines wrinkling the corners of his very blue eyes to Pan-like brilliance.

'Oh, I didn't mean – I didn't mean you. I meant—' What *did* she mean exactly? The truth was simple; she meant, 'How funny, how odd that I could so unexpectedly meet such a marvellous person, someone I could passionately love just like my gipsy girl with Sir Robert Tyzackass, only more so! – *real*.' Yes, that was it, only naturally she couldn't tell him or even put it into words herself. So she said with a spurt of inspiration which was half the truth '—It was your name. Blakey.'

'Yes?'

'I used to write things when I was young, *very* young,' she explained in her most mature manner, 'and I sent a story to a publisher. His name was Blakey, too.'

'Now that's interesting, Priscilla – I may call you Priscilla, mayn't I?' She nodded, and he continued. 'You're probably

73

referring to my very learned brother. He's a publisher with offices in London. Vigo Street.'

Her eyes widened. 'That's it. Vigo Street.' Her face which had brightened with interest, sobered quickly, as though a cloud had shadowed the sunshine.

'And was your story published?'

She shook her head, glancing down at her sandy toes.

'No. It wasn't very good. But he, Mr Blakey, wrote me a very nice letter.'

'Nice letters can be a bore if they don't say what they want. Still, it's early days yet. You're only a—'

'Child?' she interrupted. 'Is that what you think? That I couldn't *possibly* write anything worthwhile?'

'I didn't say that.'

'No, but you thought it, didn't you? And I'm not so *very* young. Do you know how old I am?'

He observed her for a moment or two so closely she could feel her spine stiffening. It was as though he was seeing right into her, piercing through clothes, flesh, and body to her very soul; and during the pause she knew that something was already being sealed between them – a bond of intuitive knowledge and desire that might eventually bridge any obstacles, given the chance. That first wild, astonished interview was one that would endure for a long time in their hearts.

'Well,' she persisted, 'please tell me.'

'I think,' he said, 'that you're tremendously old. As old as Eve, and young as the dawn. Does that satisfy you.'

'Not really. But it sounds poetical.'

'Oh, I'm no poet, I can assure you. And I certainly wouldn't stick my neck out making a guess at any lady's age, even a budding authoress like you.'

'You're laughing at me.'

'Yes. And do you know why?'

'No.'

'Because it's so refreshing meeting someone unscathed by the world. An innocent, that's what you are. An unusual commodity these days.'

'You sound bitter. Are you bitter, Mr Blakey?'

'Sometimes,' he admitted. 'War has a nasty knack of emphasising the raw spots in one's ego. Now, for Pete's sake! What the devil's got into me, talking such morbid rot to a lovely nymph like you.'

'I don't mind,' Priscilla told him. 'Sometimes I go very serious too. And sometimes—' she glanced at him mischievously, 'I'm not serious at all, and have all kinds of wicked thoughts; well, things that are *supposed* to be wicked by people like old Perrot. She was my governess for ages, but not any more. I have a tutor now. His name's John Lord. You see my sister – my *half* sister—'

It was just at this point that discussion was ended between them by Lise appearing round a bend of the cliff. She was wearing a white dress that emphasised her flying mane of silver-gold hair and ivory sheen of skin, the pointed elfin face with the brilliant dark eyes and gleam of perfect teeth between the tilted lips.

She stopped abruptly in front of them, gave a little gasp of pleasure, and exclaimed, 'Ah!' to her sister. 'You have a – a friend, yes?' And looking directly at Jason, 'You are friend, monsieur?'

Priscilla's heart sank. Just like Lise, she thought with a wave of irritation, to barge in, pushing herself forward at the worst possible time. Why had she to do it? Just when she and Jason Blakey were getting on so well. Everything would be different now, because the whole atmosphere was spoiled. Something secret and very lovely had been broken, something that might never be mended or happen again.

Feeling utterly miserable she heard Jason reply, 'I certainly hope so.' He was staring hard at Lise, but it was impossible to say from his expression what he thought of the ethereal-looking creature confronting him.

No one could possibly deny her beauty. But perhaps he didn't like fair people, Priscilla told herself hopefully. And anyway Lise was only twelve, whereas she, Priscilla, was almost fifteen, quite a young lady when properly dressed, her stepmother had told her only recently. So she braced herself to say in a sedate manner of which Miss Perrot would *certainly* have approved:

'Well, Mr Blakey, I'm sure you're busy, and Lise and I should be going back to the house. Papa doesn't care for us to be out alone for too long, and it's been ages already.'

She took Lise's arm. The child shook herself free. 'Non. Not *me*. You – yes. But papa told me to run away and find you. So?'

After a quizzical glance at Priscilla's expression, Jason said, 'Your sister is right, I think, and it's true I have things to do. But we'll meet again, never fear. Your father has invited me to dinner one night. I shall accept the invitation with great pleasure, and stipulate or rather request that you're both there.'

'That will be lovely,' Priscilla said, suddenly smiling radiantly. 'All right. Goodbye, then, until – until—'

'I see you at Mooncarn, or perhaps earlier.'

He lifted a hand in a quick wave as the two girls walked away, Lise grudgingly, Priscilla with a joyous singing sensation in her brain and heart. 'Let it be earlier,' she thought. 'Sometime when Lise is with Perrot.'

But she had no glance of Jason again until almost a week had passed, when he arrived for the meal with the family. She'd managed two solitary visits to the cove and adjoining harbour hoping to 'bump into him' apparently casually, doing something to his boat or talking to fishermen mingling with other natives round the jetty. But he hadn't been there. His yacht lay secured safely lying to one side, on a dry patch of sand glistening fresh with new paint in the sunshine. Lonely looking somehow, Priscilla thought, as lonely as she suddenly felt. And that was strange, that she could feel so dismal, so bereft, when the sky was so gloriously blue and the sun warm and spreading its mellow golden light over cliffs, pale sand, and the froth of foam from breaking waves.

On each occasion she'd wandered about a bit before making her way back to Mooncarn. Once climbing the steep narrow street of Wynk, she'd thought she'd seen him ahead, talking to a woman. She'd hurried until she was breathless, and her forehead and neck shone with damp beads of perspiration that trickled down her bare brown young arms. But when she reached the couple she found she was mistaken. Only the colour of the man's hair resembled Jason's, and something about his build. Well, perhaps it was a good thing, she thought following the first disappointment. She must be looking what old Perrot would have called 'an untidy mess', and she wouldn't have known what to say to him anyway, except that she was pleased he was coming to dinner the following Tuesday. Supposing he'd said, 'Am I? It's possible, but I *may* have been called away before that,' or something of the kind. All things considered, she decided, it was best to take her father's word about the arrangement, and not appear as though she was running after him.

The special evening arrived at last. William, who at that period had niggling business problems to face, had managed to forget them for the time being, and was in vast good humour to meet the young brother of Edward Blakey, an acquaintance of his who was concerned in publishing a record of the progress of shipping during the last hundred years. William also was considering giving reasonable backing financially to young Jason's ambition for his company, recently formed, which had at the moment only two ships for trading. With industry and foreign trade ever expanding, shipping, properly handled, could be a lucrative business, and Jason from what he'd heard was an adventurous courageous young fellow who'd fought well for his country, and in his earlier youth had travelled quite extensively, proving he had initiative and the true mariner's capacity to captain his own craft if necessary.

So the meeting from the first moment the two men faced each other was amicable and forthright. Cook had prepared a mouth-watering meal from suggestions gleaned from a magazine providing tips by a Mrs Beeton, who a few years later was to become famous for her book on *Household Management*. Olivia, looking resplendently mature, yet also invitingly coquettish in olive green silk trimmed by cream braid, made a flattering yet dignified hostess, conversing only at tactful periods when the occasion demanded it, but with her long eyes appraisingly warm on this surprisingly youthful and handsome acquaintance of her ageing husband. Jason, on his part, was quick to sense her underlying hunger for admiration, and gave it in a subtle manner that could in no way affront William.

The two girls, each in their different ways appearing quite charming, were mostly silent, but at moments Priscilla recognised a friendly glint in his glance towards her which was almost conspiratorial. Once, he even winked – just a slight movement of one eye which thrilled her and went unnoticed by the others. Her heart was beating quickly beneath the soft gold shade of her best dress. At Olivia's instigation and support, she had been allowed to have her hair parted in the centre, plaited and pinned in coils to the back of her head. Lise on the other hand was wearing green muslin with her pale hair falling softly on either side of her face. She looked quite exquisite, but despite her sidelong glances towards Jason, watched closely by Priscilla, appeared to evoke no particular attention from him.

Miss Perrot, who did not approve of the two girls being formal on such an adult occasion, had chosen to eat in her own room from a tray delivered by the maidservant. 'I'm doing my very best to bring up Miss Lise free of sophisticated society, to remain her own lovely young self,' she'd complained to Cook, 'but that woman, the *mistress*, seems determined to undermine my authority. What can I *do*?' She'd lifted both hands helplessly. 'Priscilla has been a young madam from the start. I'm free of her now, thank goodness. But *Lise*—' she broke off in frustration.

Cook, who was used to such outbursts from the poor thwarted spinster from time to time and could be relied upon to keep her tongue, had merely remarked, 'In my opinion, Miss Lise will develop in her own way because she hasn't the imagination to do any other. You just do your best, Miss Perrot, and let the future take care of itself. That's the only commonsense way to look at things. After all—' She'd hesitated before pointing out, 'S'long as the master's satisfied, that's all that matters.'

'Not to me,' came the prim reply. 'My charge's welfare is a duty.'

'Duty? Hm! well, duty can be a hard taskmaster sometimes, and that's for sure.'

Silence had followed the brief passage of words, and Miss Perrot relieved, if not satisfied, by her own display of irritation had been able to assume a more philosophical attitude by telling herself that the young handsome man she'd seen from the top of the stairs entering the hall, would probably not be in the locality for much longer. She'd heard from the daily maid that he was setting sail very shortly for foreign faraway parts, so there was every chance he would be unable to make a second visit to Mooncarn. For some instinctive reason that she couldn't 'put a finger on', as the saying went, she didn't trust him. It never occurred to her that jealousy might play a part in her feelings, jealousy of the Clinton girls' budding adolescence, and most of all, of Olivia's blatant sexuality, of the subtle swing of hips when any presentable male was around, and a hidden erotic awareness in the governess Maud Perrot's being, of Jason Blakey's inevitable response.

However, further pondering over the question of Jason Blakey did not arise, for what the daily maid had prophesied came true. Jason had to leave Plynport on a business matter — concerning his newly formed shipping project, William said — at a moment's notice, and no-one at Mooncarn saw him again before leaving.

Priscilla felt desolate, assuming that although he'd liked her — yes, she knew that was true — he had, after all, regarded her as no more than a child who couldn't possibly have any serious thoughts about a man such as himself, an adventurer of twenty-five, with years of experience, including the tragic Balaclava incident, behind him.

*

During the next two years, William's business and creative projects became more widespread, taking more tax of his physical and mental ability than he realised. The life-style imposed on him since his marriage to Olivia demanded an ever-increasing income to keep his bank balance on an even keel. Profits gradually sank, even showing a debit in unexpected quarters. The loss of £25,000 through having to fork out the sum demanded when the Northern construction plan failed, had sapped temporarily all initiative from him.

His wealth had not suffered too badly, but the first frail doubt he'd ever had concerning his judgement on an enterprising scheme niggled at his mind and brain, throwing him, after the first initial shock, into a fever of ruthless application to work that left him frequently tense and sleepless, and unable to concentrate the following day with his usual rational capacity.

He began to look his age. Though still a handsome man his complexion became florid, the indication of a paunch showed, and there were bags under his fine eyes. He was at times irritable, though he did his best never to show this to the girls. But Olivia became bored. His charm was waning, he seldom paid her the compliments she was used to, and demanded. The ardour and fire of his glance during their less frequent intimate moments was dulled, or not there at all. He drank more heavily than he used to, and it was clear to Priscilla that her father was not well.

William had taken in as junior partner a Captain Frederick Challoner, on whom he seemed to rely a good deal. Priscilla neither liked nor completely trusted him, though he was polite, clever, handsome and with an extremely enterprising brain, charming manners, and a witty tongue. She had met him many times, he was so often at number 7, and always he'd made himself attentive. But there was something about him — what was it? Her bright youthful brain searched for the word and found it. Suave. Yes, that was it — he was too suave to be quite true.

Olivia, to the contrary, fanned herself in the glow of his flattery which was like warm sunshine to her starved ego.

A day came in 1858 shortly before Priscilla's eighteenth birthday when William had to face the unpleasant truth that if matters did not improve he would either have to declare himself bankrupt or salvage what assets he had to pay debts, and move from Seagrave Square to living in considerably more modest circumstances at Mooncarn. He knew this was possible, but dreaded the effect of such a state of affairs upon his family, especially Olivia.

Trustingly, he confided his fears and any alternative course that lay open, to Challoner. The captain ridiculed William's assessment of the situation with jovial light-hearted contempt that might have deceived a less astute character than William Clinton.

'Stuff and nonsense,' he exclaimed. 'Sheer bunkum, Will. You've lost sight of payments due and what should come from the Westgate Commission. Then that Cathedral design, and the new steamship—'

'I've never banked on what's *supposed* to come in,' William interrupted heavily, 'or on dreams that haven't matured. How the hell I got into this position beats me. Don't you realise what it means, man? Or haven't you studied the books recently?'

'I leave that to the accountants. They're paid for doing the job.'

'Yes,' William agreed, 'and a fine old muddle they seem to be in at the moment. I just *don't understand*.'

And indeed he didn't. He trusted his business staff, but there was obviously something very wrong somewhere. He couldn't accept that Olivia's extravagance alone had led him into such straits. Another worrying point was that he'd failed in securing certain important contracts after delivering ingenious and completely practical designs for the projects in question, only to find that he was too late. Similar ideas had already been put before the firms involved, and accepted. This was not only extremely frustrating, but odd, decidedly odd, because he happened to be an individualist whose work always bore a personal stamp. Could there be a leak somewhere? An underground sneak-thief stealing the fruit of his brain for his own benefit? Such a thought was not only highly obnoxiously unpleasant, but extremely distressing. The only direct confidante with access to his most intimate plans was Challoner himself, and it was to the captain's benefit they should prosper. Unless – but he dismissed any festering wild doubts as mere fantasy. Not only would his faith in human nature be shocked beyond belief should Challoner prove to be a snake in the grass, but for the man to succeed in becoming one would be too intricate and risky.

But apart from the captain, who else? If indeed it was so? Could he himself, William Clinton, have become careless during the last year or two? Sufficiently careless over his brandy, in dropping a word here and there in the club, which provided the bridge to betrayal? One by one suggestions brooded in his brain until they finally disintegrated leaving him exhausted and uncertain of his own judicial capacity for the first time in his life.

However, steeling his nerve to face any forthcoming possibility, he pulled himself together sufficiently to assume a facade of well-being for Priscilla's eighteenth birthday party which was to be held at Seagrave Square regardless of expense, to demonstrate the deep love and devotion he had for his eldest child. The celebration in a sense, would serve a double purpose, for during that same week of October, Blakeys the publishers were bringing out a travel book dealing with a round-the-world tour made by a schooner, which had been designed by William Clinton, and captained by a member of the Blakey family, Jason, one of the surviving heroes of Balaclava.

The dedication was to William, which would enhance his prestige, if not his pocket. The book was not expected to be a 'best seller' in a business sense, but doubtless collectors and those with seafaring and explorative interests would be eager to add the volume to their shelves. The publishers were confident of making a modest profit, and taking all things into consideration the event was worthy of a toast. So arrangements were made for the occasion.

A list of guests included Alexander Stern, eldest son and heir to Lord Stern of Stonewell, wealthy owner of estates in Cornwall, Leicestershire and a mansion in Belgravia. Alex had met Priscilla on several occasions, and the rich, quite attractive but easy-going young man known to be a connoisseur of women, though something of a playboy, had shown considerable interest in the aloof proud-looking girl who from the beginning of their contact had treated him casually as though he was merely any ordinary acquaintance, of no particular importance in her life. This was quite true, of course. Priscilla was impressed neither by riches nor the fact that by most girls of her age she would be envied. Alex was a catch, as Olivia had pointed out to her more than once. The girl had laughed lightly and said, 'I know. But I don't want him falling in front of me.'

'Don't you like him? He appears most attentive and pleasant to me, and no one can say he isn't handsome.'

Priscilla had shrugged. 'Oh, he's all right. Yes. I like him in a way. He can be fun, I suppose, but I couldn't ever – well, you know, think of him in any *serious* way.'

'That's a pity, my dear,' Olivia had replied. 'I wouldn't make up your mind yet to say no, if he should ask you.'

'Whatever do you *mean*?'

Olivia's almond-shaped eyes had been very steady and meaningful on her step-daughter's face when she'd said, 'Diamonds don't grow on bushes, gold doesn't sprout in every man's pockets, *and* – there's your father.'

Priscilla's luminous eyes had widened with astonishment. '*Papa?* What has papa to do with Alex?'

'Don't say you haven't noticed how he's changed lately. He's worried, and losing his grip on things.'

Priscilla frowned. What Olivia said was true. He'd been abstracted recently, and on the rare occasions when he'd relaxed with his glass beside him, she'd been aware of the sagging flesh under the eyes and jaw line, how tired he looked, too tired even to respond or take interest in family matters. He had smiled less, too. It was as though the strength and vitality which had always been so characteristic of William Clinton was slowly being sapped away.

'He's been working very hard,' Priscilla had replied doubtfully. 'I thought that was it. Anyway I don't see where Alex Stern comes into it.'

'Don't you? Then use your brain. Knowing his favourite daughter was secure for the rest of her life might take a load of worry from him.'

'*No*.' Priscilla's voice was definite. 'Papa would hate me to marry anyone I didn't love, and if you're suggesting he has money troubles, I don't believe it. If he had it would show in lots of ways; he'd *say*. But perhaps — perhaps he ought to see a doctor.'

'You just suggest that to him, and a fine response you'd get,' Olivia said bitterly. 'Can you imagine William Clinton facing a medical man and saying, "Can you help me, I've been feeling rather tired lately?" Oh, no. I can assure you it's something more tangible than pills and potions he's in need of.'

After that conversation, however, it had appeared that William's ebullience was beginning to reassert itself. He had put on a facade of well-being, and with the approach of the forthcoming party and publication of *Round the World*, only a keen observer could have detected that he was not his own self. A little more aged perhaps, his friends said, but that was all — the natural toll of passing years. Priscilla was only too relieved to accept this view, and rid herself of Olivia's pessimistic comments.

As for Lise, she was too concerned with herself to bother much about anyone or anything else. The awkwardness of adolescence had passed her by. Her beauty if possible had increased and become more dramatic. She could have been some fantastic creation stepped into the present, from an extravagant French Court of a bygone period or a dainty enchantress from Perrault or de la Motte. Inherently she was a born coquette. Charming males, and ruffling women, came as naturally to her as eating or sleeping. She had no nerves or imagination, and it was only when any individual came to know her well that the truth emerged — she had not the heart to feel anything deeply. Usually she was well-behaved and sweet-tempered, but at puberty she had developed a propensity for scowling with a quick stamp of one pretty foot if she did not instantly obtain anything she wanted.

Yet in spite of such shortcomings, Priscilla had developed a certain fondness for her, perhaps because she sensed that unless protected that glorious cloud of pale hair and lovely face alone could not bring happiness. Lise would never know the beauty and the pain of loving or being loved. There would never be any Jason in her life, no-one to whom she could turn and say honestly, 'I love you. I would die for you.'

Of course, most people would say such a statement was ridiculous, but Priscilla herself knew such dangerous emotions could be true, just as she knew that one day she must meet Jason Blakey again. Ever since their encounter almost three years ago, she had thought about him intermittently, remembered the pledge given in that long look before parting. He'd made light of things – well, that was natural. She'd been little more than a child then, and he'd had his job to do, sailing the world. But she'd never doubted that chance or the Fates must one day bring them together. In the meantime, she'd enjoyed life, written a few poems, and modified *The Adventures of Sir Robert Tyzackass* to more acceptable and adult reading. She was excited to know that the publisher, Jason's brother, whom she'd written to those years ago would be at the party, though disappointed it couldn't be Jason himself.

'A likable young fellow, Jason, and a real adventurer,' her father had told her. 'But apparently he has other business on. A pity. You two got on well, I remember.'

'Yes,' Priscilla had replied. 'Still,' shrugging her shoulders, 'it will be pleasant meeting your Mr Blakey. I'll look forward to that.'

She meant to behave in her most dignified manner when they were introduced, she decided, and perhaps, just *perhaps*, if he was pleasant and not too remote a character or frighteningly knowledgeable, she might reveal herself to him as 'Cornelia Almond', just for the interest and fun of seeing his reaction – that is, if he remembered her youthful effort at all.

So preparations for the celebration continued, with numerous little side-issues imbuing the affair with a more than usual interest. Even the servants' quarters were agog with gossip. Whispers had somehow got around that Lord Stern's son, the Honourable Alexander was about to ask the master for Miss Priscilla's hand in marriage. It was said also that Miss Lise was bound to interfere and try and grab him for herself.

'If she does, good luck to her, and to us,' Cook said sourly. 'But you're all talking nonsense; Miss Lise is only just sixteen, and no brains in her head yet – none at all. As for Miss Priscilla, she's more sense than to get hitched up with such a vain weak-kneed creature. Oh, he's good looking enough, I grant you that. But no real guts, and a fly-by-night into the bargain. So don't go putting such silly tales about. The next thing I'll be hearing I s'pose is that Captain Challoner's got his eye on her.'

The head kitchen maid winked at the junior footman. 'Reckon he's looking in other quarters,' she said, with a sly grimace.

'Madam, d'you mean?'

'I wouldn't say "yes", and I wouldn't say "no",' came the ambiguous reply. 'But you just watch out. It wouldn't surprise me at *all* if something scandalous didn't happen any day.'

'And unless you watch your words you'll get a box on the ear,' Cook remarked sharply. 'So attend to your work.'

The housekeeper, Mrs Prout, entered the kitchen at that moment. She glanced round enquiringly. 'Is anything wrong, Cook?'

'No, Mrs Prout, I was just speaking my mind that's all. Sometimes it's necessary if work's to be done as it should be.'

'Quite right. I agree with you. I commend you for keeping order.'

With a rustle of black silk the tall thin figure departed, and Cook, with a warning glance at the kitchen maid, recommenced her preparations for that evening's menu.

The day of the much-discussed event arrived at last. In the morning Priscilla received her gifts — jewellery from her father, flowers and numerous extravagantly attractive articles, including a delicately ornate fan from Olivia, and a brooch chosen also by her stepmother, but ostensibly from her half-sister, Lise.

The immensely wide hall was decorated by coloured hanging Japanese lanterns swung across the ceiling, and by palms and potted plants brought in from the conservatory. The brilliant room, in which the green velvety-topped table looked minute compared with the vast size of the interior, had been cleared for dancing, except in the alcove at the far end where a fire spluttered from the wide grate, and a line of seating under the three Gothic-style windows was prepared, intended for dowagers and any exhausted female who wished to collapse momentarily with her smelling salts and fan.

In the dining room the larger refectory table under the hatch was laid early with glinting silver and glass; a second table for drinks, to be supervised by the butler, stood ready. The large conservatory inner door had been opened hours before the proceedings started, allowing the aroma of blossoming exotic plants to pervade the air and also, of course, for the use of young couples anxious to indulge in a little flirtatious romance. The powder closet, very near the largest lounge and drawing-room, had been prepared as an attractive retiring room. Everything had been arranged as conveniently as possible, including the music for which William had hired a trio to perform from the music room opening directly into the vast hall.

William had made certain that his study was to be used only for male cronies wishing for a smoke and brief escape from feminine company.

On the face of it, therefore, it appeared that nothing could possibly go wrong. Indeed, the indications were that something exceedingly romantic and to the advantage of the Clinton establishment was hovering tantalisingly on the horizon. The servants' predictions had been very near the truth.

During the morning an immense intricate flower arrangement had been delivered and carried to the small lounge where presents were on view, addressed to 'my dear Priscilla, from her friend and admirer, Alex'. The attached gold-embossed card bore the Stern crest. Even Priscilla was impressed, and more so when a servant handed her a small box encased in silvered paper which also bore her name.

'This came with the flowers, Miss Priscilla.'

When the footman had retired, Priscilla opened the gift, staring in astonishment, amazement, and a certain niggling apprehension. She took the lid off cautiously, and there, soft in its bed of cottonwool was a gleaming pendant − one immense diamond set in a filigree of gold.

'But *why*?' she gasped. 'For me? − it can't be. There must be some mistake.'

Her father, who was standing nearby with Olivia and Lise, beamed on her. 'Of course it's for you, love. Put it on, try it.'

'But I don't understand—'

'My dear girl, what did I tell you?' Olivia remarked, stepping forward and helping fasten the clasp round the slim neck. 'Alexander's in love with you; this proves it. A mark of his esteem and affection. You're a very lucky young woman.'

'That's right, child,' William confirmed, 'providing you return his feelings, of course. I wouldn't—'

'She will, when she thinks about it, and gets to know him better,' Olivia interrupted. 'At this point, all Priscilla has to do when the young man arrives is to express her deep gratitude and be seen wearing the pendant.'

Priscilla's hand went to her neck protestingly. '*No*, I *won't* wear it tonight. I've the necklace papa gave me, the one with the pearls in it. It will go better with my dress. Besides, if I wore this it would look as though I was — already promised.' Her voice held just a touch of youthful irony. 'Everyone would think it indicated I was *fond* of Alex. It would be sort of—'

'But you *are*, aren't you? You *do like* him.'

'Oh, yes. In a way. He's fun. But that doesn't mean to say I want to show off in it. *Other* people have sent me gifts. It wouldn't be fair, would it, papa?'

William rubbed his chin reflectively, a sign that he was considering carefully before he answered, then he told his daughter, after a pause, 'Oh, I don't think fairness comes into it, love. Certainly young Alex has paid you a great compliment. By jove, yes. It would be a pity perhaps not to show your appreciation.'

Priscilla's eyes widened. 'You mean that? You think I should?'

William lowered his eyes slightly, unable to meet the challenging honesty of his daughter's clear eyes.

'It would be tactful,' he answered. 'But it's for you to decide.'

So in the end, when Priscilla, with the help of Perrot, was dressed for her birthday dinner, the immense diamond glistened just below the hollow of her throat above the shadowed curve of her breasts. Her gown was of blue tulle over pale green silk, adorned with tiny daisies, cut low on the shoulders, and tightly waisted, having a hooped skirt with just the suggestion of a train. She had had it made especially for the occasion similar to a style designed by Worth for Princess Metternich, at Olivia's instigation.

William at the time had been slightly shocked by the cost, and when shortly before the party Olivia had asked him if he did not think his daughter looked quite adorable he'd replied, 'She always looks good — *beautiful* in my eyes. Oh, yes, the dress has style. She could be any young duchess, I grant you. But after this affair, my dear, we'll have to draw in our horns. Economise a bit. I hope you realise it.'

Olivia's face had hardened. 'Fancy talking about *economy* at this point — an hour before the guests arrive. Really, William, at times you *are* rather—'

'Dull?'

'Well, inconsistent. Tonight of all nights when everyone — even you — should be feeling lively. Oh—' She shrugged her shoulders in exasperation.

'I'm sorry I bore you.' He spoke curtly. 'Forget it, for tonight. But I warn you—' He raised a finger forebodingly. 'In future there can be no more extravagance. It's serious, Olivia.'

He'd turned and left the room on heavy feet, closing the door with a sharp snap behind him. Olivia had stood motionless for a few seconds looking straight ahead, at nothing in particular, but with a stormy, condemning look in her narrowed gaze. Little her husband could have guessed the relentless purpose behind her rigid facade, the contempt for his decreasing 'drive', and the waning of the energy that she'd at first so admired in him. The greying man with tired eyes and portly bulge beneath the elegant waistcoat was not the William Clinton she'd married. He had lost his fire and grit, and Olivia despised failure.

Nevertheless, she put on a determined front of harmony and greeted the guests smilingly beside her husband as they were ushered in, after capes, bonnets and top hats and coats had been removed by the servant in attendance, and the ladies taken to the powder closet.

Priscilla stood just in the entrance to the drawing room with Lise lingering close by. Lise in deep pink had the appearance of some beautiful rose about to burst into full floom. It was she, with her startling mane of glistening pale hair, who caught the first attention, but Priscilla to whom all eyes turned, turned and rested on, so graciously lovely was she, yet filled with glowing vitality and warmth.

At odd moments, William glanced down on her, and it was as though for a second or two the strain of years left him. He was proud of her, this girl he'd fathered. No other woman in the world, he knew, would ever mean as much to him. God help him if he ever let her down. Priscilla sensing something of what he felt, found time, even in the hubbub of the primary reception, to smile up at him, and once squeeze his hand. The next moment she was whirled up in a little crowd of new arrivals, including the Honourable Alex. She felt a wave of colour, of faint embarrassment stain her cheeks when he glanced at the shining jewel resting on her cream skin. He grinned, and Alex's grin was a natural friendly glow of satisfaction. 'Glad you got it in time,' he said. 'By jove, it suits you.'

'You shouldn't have done,' she protested, almost in a whisper. 'But thank you, Alex.'

'No need for thanks.' His voice was gruff. 'But see you save the supper dance for me.'

She nodded. 'All right.'

'Hey! let me have that.' He reached for the little card dangling with the small linked gold chain bag suspended from one mittened wrist.

'Oh, no, I—' But he managed to detach it and hastily scribbled his name all over the place on it. Then he moved away with a wink and a cheeky laugh.

Priscilla frowned, but she couldn't really be angry with him. He was so good-natured and fun when he wanted to be, but a bit of a bore. At the first available moment she scanned the card, and immediately crossed out more than half the dances he'd reserved. Then she took another and allotted three to him, which she considered was quite enough.

'That's cheating,' she heard a suave well-bred voice say behind her. She turned sharply. Captain Challoner appeared extremely smart, elegant, and fascinating in his bland dark way, and was looking down on her speculatively, a teasing smile under his well-trimmed moustache, black eyes — or so they appeared in the brilliant flash of chandeliers — noting the jewel at the base of her throat.

'You look quite — ravishing,' he continued, 'and that sparkler suits you.'

'Thank you,' she said coldly, disliking him, although she could not have said exactly why.

He gave a little bow. 'As a friend of the family, may I presume I have the liberty to ask for a dance when the time comes?'

'Perhaps, Captain Challoner,' Priscilla answered. 'I have several waltzes booked already, but the Lancers may be possible.'

His acknowledgement to her reply held a hint of sarcasm as he said, 'I'm delighted; much obliged to you, Miss Clinton.'

He turned and went to a buffet table where drinks were already being served.

As the evening wore on, following the toasting and congratulations, the atmosphere became heady, with a whirl of rustling skirts, muffled laughter and conversation, wine, perfume, warm air, and dreamy music from the trio. Like immense exotic butterflies, girls drifted through the hall and round the brilliant room to the strains of Johann Strauss's 'Blue Danube' and the Emperor Waltz, minuets, and two sets of Lancers performed in rollicking fashion in the wide main corridor.

Priscilla enjoyed her numbers with Alex, who was a good dancer, and didn't take it amiss when she restrained him from holding her too tightly. 'To the contrary,' he joked, holding her at arm's length for a second, and remarked lightly, 'Anything "your ladyship" demands.'

'Thank you, your Lordship,' Priscilla answered mockingly.

'Ah—' he whispered. Then close to her ear, so close a curl quivered intriguingly from his breath, 'Wait until the old man pops off and you're *really* a ladyship — *mine*.'

A little startled, Priscilla exclaimed, 'Don't be ridiculous, Alex.'

He stopped dancing suddenly, mopped his brow, took her arm and pulled her towards the conservatory. But seeing the little crowd inside he paused near the entrance, and looking quite serious said quietly, 'I *want* to *marry* you, Priscilla. Dammit, I've never said that to any girl before.'

'You will though,' Priscilla retorted lightly. 'Many times, I'm quite sure.'

'No. You're wrong.'

'Oh, you're just being silly. How much champagne have you drunk?'

'Listen.' His hand slid down to her delicate but firm young waist. Glancing up at him, in profile and so serious, she realised for the first time quite how handsome he was. 'I mean it,' he continued. 'I didn't intend to speak out so soon before I'd talked to your old man, but—'

Bewildered and embarrassed, she tried to free herself.

'Oh, Alex. Really! this is not the time for—'

'I know, I know. But think about it. Oh, hell, some stuffed-shirt is going to put his foot in it—'

'Bobby, Bobby Roberts,' Priscilla exclaimed quickly. 'It's his dance.'

It wasn't actually, but the white lie together with the fact that Bobby had been her humble admirer for two years and would most certainly grab the chance of partnering her, served the purpose.

Frustrated, Alex watched jealously as the graceful figure in its cloud of blue and green chiffon was whirled away through the door into the wide hall and brilliant room. He had no chance to see her alone again that night, but his mind was made up.

'Find a wife,' the pater had told him recently. 'It's about time. At twenty-five you should have sown your wild oats, and I want to see the name safe and an heir to follow on. There are plenty of well-bred fillies around; find one healthy and strong, a good breeder as well as a looker, but remember – the first's the most important. All women look alike in the dark.'

Crude advice, Alex had thought, but he supposed there was some sense in it. He hadn't been too keen on the idea of marriage, not until he'd discovered Priscilla and found also what an evasive creature she was. That she didn't care two hoots about his title or money had been obvious from the start of their relationship, and this fact alone emphasised her attraction for him. Hard to get, that was Priscilla Clinton, and he wanted her. He'd no doubt that he'd win her in the end, and that possessing both beauty and good blood, on her mother's side, the old man would be pleased.

That evening, however, something occurred that was to change the whole course of the Clinton family menage.

Priscilla — having dutifully danced a vigorous polka with Jason's brother, the publisher, who despite his fifteen years' seniority, was a sprightly character, slender and bright-eyed, with a puckish smile faintly similar to Jason's — was crossing the hall to the powder room feeling the need for cologne, when something drew her attention to a figure in the act of delivering his cape and tall hat to the attendant. No one else at that moment was about. The orchestra was taking a respite before commencing the next number which preceded the last waltz. Guests were gathered mostly round the buffet, in the drawing room, or in the conservatory. Alex, to Priscilla's relief, had been commandeered by Lise who wore the entrancing innocent look which by many matrons was called 'coy' or 'forward'. But obviously Alex had been taken off his guard, and although she might not have been to his taste, he was quite clearly curious concerning the 'brainless and precocious' child who, although frowned on by so many mothers, was such a fascinating little beauty.

For once, Priscilla was wildly grateful to her half-sister, because, when the newcomer turned and came towards her, with a brilliant gleam of light catching his face from a flickering wall chandelier, she saw that the lurch of her heart had not deceived her. The late guest was — 'oh, darling, darling' — she thought breathlessly, whispering unbelievingly — *'Jason'*.

'Hallo, Priscilla,' he smiled, and the years fell away. Memory swept them both. He was on a pale, lonely shore and his eyes were on hers, the same intense blue eyes, more blue than the summer skies over Mooncarn, and filled with the recognition they'd both felt on that far off day, but it was different now, because she was older, grown up, and there was no obstacle any more, nothing to keep them apart.

He shook his head wonderingly. 'You look — my dear love! oh, my sweet, wild love—' He glanced round. 'Is there anywhere we can go?'

'The gazebo. There'll be no one there. They're getting ready for the last dance, and it's not lighted. Come — quickly—'

In her pointed pale blue satin slippers with her skirt lifted in both hands above her ankles and taffeta petticoat, she sped down the narrowing hallway towards the servants' quarters and disappeared into an alcove from where a side door led into the garden, followed by Jason.

After the heat, the air was cool, still lit by a pale moon in the velvet sky, though dawn would soon be spreading a line of silver on the far horizon. They hurried breathlessly through the violet-black shadows of bushes and clipped trees, heedless of the fact that Priscilla's absence might soon be noted, conscious only of each other, of the strange magical awareness of two beings brought together again by destiny, will, or the fates that had proved the impossible could be true — the child and man of yesterday had known it from the beginning. They were lovers for all time. But she was a woman now, and ripe for living.

He took her in his arms, and his lips warm and ardent, yet sweet with adoration, were on her own. Her slender body was crushed against his, their two hearts pounding with the tumult of desire and longing. 'Oh, I *love* you, Jason,' she murmured, with her curls tumbled against his shoulders. 'I've dreamed of this — so often. But I never thought—'

'Yes, you did, you *knew* — you witch. It's true, isn't it?' For a second he released her sufficiently to see deep into her clear shining pools of eyes where all the promise of their future was written, heralding a tie strong enough to withstand any conceivable obstacle — even death.

How long he held her there, lusting with his senses, yet worshipping her more, they never knew.

When they returned to the house, the guests were departing. The last dying strains of the waltz had faded, and Alex had already left.

So had others.

But no one realised until later that Olivia and Captain Challoner had also gone, eloped secretly in his cab which was waiting discreetly in the shadows of a side drive.

Priscilla's birthday party was over.

4

It was not until the following morning that the household became fully aware of Olivia's absence. Jason had returned alone to the house the previous evening, on the pretext of making a brief contact and apologies to William for his absence, then departed immediately with his brother. Priscilla had wandered down the hall nonchalantly a moment or two later, bright-eyed, with cheeks flushed, just as the last couples were departing. William had glanced at her enquiringly, but was too irritable and tired to make any direct questioning.

Olivia! Where the deuce was she, he'd thought, and why hadn't she had the decency to make a show of politeness by his side when the guests left? He'd a shrewd idea where Priscilla had been, and although she'd doubtless had a secret little liaison with young Jason she could have chosen a better moment. Mostly, though, he didn't blame her. She was young and emotional, and if romance was in the air, let her have a spot. She'd danced a good bit with Alex, too. Now a match there would please him. Might help to ease his financial problems considerably. He got on well with the sporting old man — the lord. Had done a large construction job for the estate in the past, and they'd had many a convivial meeting together. There'd been no doubt in William's mind that Priscilla, as Stern's daughter-in-law, would be warmly welcomed; any man would be proud to have her in the family, and if necessary he felt certain that the wealthy aristocrat wouldn't grudge putting his hand in his pocket to help tide over the network of difficulties confronting the Clinton business. It would only be a loan. William would pay it back. He was proud. But by God, when he was clear of debt, he'd see that Olivia toed the line, and cut her coat according to *his* cloth. He'd been weak, a fool with her. And he'd see too that she kept free of Challoner. Something had been going on between them he'd felt sure of it, just as he was ninety-nine and a half per cent certain that Challoner had been lining his own pocket at *his*, William's, expense. Oh, the man had been clever; too clever to prove anything, yet, in black and white. But in time he'd have the evidence and then out he would go, to face the consequences, which could mean criminal charges and a trial.

In the meantime, he'd see that wife of his learned her place. There'd be no chance in the future for those sly glances between the two, for her provocative smile at the handsome snake he'd taken in as partner. It hadn't escaped him, and many times lately he'd been on the point of challenging her, but because of his worries and lack of fire due to tiredness, he'd put the matter off, till he felt his own self again.

Besides, there'd been Priscilla to think of. Any violent scene before her party — and there'd been occasion when Olivia had roused the desire in him to strike her — would have effectively disillusioned and shattered the child's happiness, as well as ruining the chance, just the *chance*, of discovering he was wrong, that the captain after all was friend not foe, and that the idea of an affair between him and Olivia had been a fantastic illusion, due to stress and worry.

Yes, he'd gone on hoping to the very last, to the moment when he'd retired exhausted to his bedroom and found on the dressing table, the note which ran:

William, I'm sorry it has to be this way but I'm leaving you. For some time now there's been no happiness between us. There are things I must have which you can no longer give me. Frederick and I have grown fond of each other, and have decided to make a complete break and live abroad. If you wish to divorce me you can have full evidence; if you don't it will make little difference to me. I'm grateful for the first days following our marriage, but it was cloud cuckoo land, wasn't it? You were really only married to your business. Perhaps I *knew* secretly, but thought I could face it for the benefits it gave me. But I can't, William. The thought of having to struggle financially with you, and live — as you suggested once, and again tonight — in reduced circumstances at that benighted place Mooncarn would have been hell to me.

Try not to think badly of me. I wish you well. So incidentally, does the captain, and don't try and involve him in your business fiasco. He has had what was his due.

                    With best wishes,
                    Olivia.

For quite a minute, perhaps more, after reading the letter, William had sat rigid, staring into space, with the sheet of paper crumpled up in one hand. His face was grey first, then crimson deepening slowly to dull purple. A nerve at one side of his mouth was twitching. He tried to take a full breath to still the sudden heavy thudding of his heart, and reached for a chair. But his lungs seemed unable to expand, and the room became a blur of thickening, whirling darkness through which he struggled vainly for sight and air.

He'd tottered for a few seconds, knocking a side table over. Then he fell.

The sound of the crash brought a manservant hurrying to the scene. Priscilla arrived a moment later. William was lying on his back, his head twisted to one side, unconscious, but still alive. He was breathing stertorously, and a trickle of blood coursed down one temple from a broken glass lying nearby. The fingers of one hand were still clutched round the crumpled letter.

The doctor was called immediately and gave his opinion that Mr Clinton had suffered a seizure from which, with luck and good nursing, he could live and ultimately possibly recover.

A specialist endorsed this opinion a few hours later, but it was not until another day had passed that William Clinton recovered consciousness, and then it was to find that he was blind.

*

Priscilla was devastated. A fortnight of anguish, hope, and despair passed during which the most eminent specialists and surgeons were called to examine her father, and the general

98

agreement was that nothing could be done for the stricken man except to ensure, if possible, that he had no worries and should be enabled to recuperate and be cared for at some place where he would be untroubled by many visitors or reminded too forcibly of his disablement. There was every chance, given time, that sight might return, and he would be enabled to live an ordinary life.

An ordinary life! William Clinton? Priscilla thought despairingly, but they didn't know him, these specialists, who however brilliant they might be at diagnosis, seemed to ignore or be unaware of the nature of their patient. Sight had been the very essence of William's life, the vision of land and sea and sky, of vast schemes dealing with the earth, and massive buildings rising from his creative capacity – the fruit of a dreamer's mind possessing the practical force to bring them into being. How could he bear it? He couldn't surely – he would die.

Sensing her distress, William, after the first shock, arrested his will and told all with stony decision on his face and in his voice, 'It isn't the end of the world, or of me. They haven't written me off yet. I can still think and move and plan. And you heard what that last fellow said, the Harley Street man; there's a chance my eyes will work again. Well, girl, we'll have to work on that. A matter of time probably, he said, didn't he—?'

'Yes, but the other one – the—'

'Oh, he was a dreary devil. Talked a lot of morbid ballyhoo. Got a name for it. That's the way they make their money – first the droning and moaning, and then when recovery comes after a session of pills and tests they take the credit for it. I shall be *all right*, Prissy. I've *got* to be. Remember what caused it – shock following this business muddle, and Olivia—'

'She's the *cause* of it,' Priscilla said. 'I *hate* her. How *could* she? And *my* party, too—'

'No, no.' William put out a hand. She gave him hers, and he grasped it firmly. 'You mustn't hate her, love. I knew what she was when I married her. I've been too soft, that's all. With Challoner, too. Between them they've made a fool of me. A fool of William Clinton.' His face paled, became grey, his fine eyes black and staring into a world he could no longer see.

'Papa—'

'It's all right, love. Get me a chair. I must rest a bit. And then, as soon as possible, when I've got — my bearings more—' a wry smile curled his lips — 'we'll go for a spell to Mooncarn, a good long one. You wouldn't mind, would you?' He felt for an arm of the chair and eased himself into it.

'Mind?' She shook her head. 'I'd like it. I love it there.'

'And how do you think Lise will feel?'

'As long as Lise can dress up and have someone admiring her, I don't think she feels much at all,' Priscilla answered honestly, but with an underlying sadness in her voice.

'No.' William sighed. 'I expect you're right. We can keep Perrot on, of course. But some of the staff will have to go.'

'For good, do you mean?'

'I'm afraid so, love. Challoner has played ducks and drakes with finances — at least that's how it appears. Whether it can ever be proved is another matter. And honestly I don't know whether it's worth trying. So long as I can square my debts and have enough to live on—' He broke off uncertainly.

'Of *course* you will,' Priscilla said, with forced vigour. 'I don't suppose things are half so bad as you imagine. As for Seagrave Square, I don't care if we leave it for good. Mooncarn's much more—'

'Remote and romantic?'

Grateful at least that the rich wave of colour to her cheeks was not obvious, and because with a sudden sense of joy that momentarily dispelled tragedy, Priscilla was picturing Jason, recalling he had a cottage near Wynk and that meetings would be so much more frequent in the future, she said gently, softly, 'Yes, romantic.'

'You like that young man, Jason Blakey, don't you?'

'Yes,' she admitted, wanting to confide more, but doubting the time was ripe, and recognising that William's blindness might delay any wild plan she'd had of an early marriage.

'And Alex? Alex Stern? How do you feel about him?'

'Oh, he's — he's fun,' Priscilla answered ambiguously. 'Yes, I like him too.'

'Hm.' William paused before continuing, 'You'd be secure with Alex. There'd be no worrying about whether you had what you deserve in life. And the old man's fond of you—'

'Yes, but—'

William's eyes turned on her unseeingly. 'What, love? But what?'

'Oh, nothing. Don't fret about me. Don't think about any-thing *at all* at the moment but getting better. *Please*, papa.'

He heaved a sigh, and got to his feet. 'Think I'll have a breath of fresh air, Prissy. Like to come? Just a stroll round the garden?'

He had been moved from the room upstairs to his study on the ground floor, which had been converted to a temporary bedroom. It had French windows opening on to the garden where a path led past a large greenhouse to a side lawn.

The afternoon was golden and still, with all the bitter-sweet earthy smells of autumn lingering in the quiet air. William, after the first few steps refused his daughter's arm. 'Got to get about on my own,' he said, tapping the ground before him with his white stick. 'As long as I can reach the arbour without break-ing my neck it'll be quite an accomplishment, eh?'

He laughed falsely, a sound echoed by Priscilla, who felt briefly that her heart was breaking.

Memories swept her as they entered the gazebo – memories so wild and sweet and poignant, that a faint mist of dizziness clouded her eyes. The sunlight was low, throwing long golden beams directly on the small retreat where such a short time ago she'd lain close in Jason's arms. A blackbird piped from an old elm tree close by. A song of hope, was it? Or premonition? Who could tell? She shivered slightly.

'What is it, Prissy?' William enquired sharply. 'Are you cold?' She'd forgotten how, since losing his sight, his other senses had become so sharpened.

'No, papa, no,' she assured him. 'There was something on my neck. A spider, I think – or perhaps a moth.'

'You were always frightened by moths, weren't you?' William said. 'Could never understand why, and yet as a little thing you'd let a spider climb your arm and not mind a bit.'

101

'Fancy remembering that,' Priscilla answered. 'Yes, it's true. And butterflies — I *love* them. But it's the way moths flap in your face with their furry wings and fat bodies. Oh, I'm silly, I know. But I just can't *stand* them.'

'We all have our pet hates,' William remarked. And just for a second his mind lurched, remembering Challoner. He hated *him*; yes, by God, he did. Not for the stealing of his wife merely — that had just been the last straw — but for purloining his dreams and most probably destroying forever his capacity to see another one fulfilled.

He did his best at that time to stifle his feelings, the hopelessness that frequently possessed him, in front of the girls, indeed from the world in general, which was a small one, just then.

Except for strolls round the garden and an occasional ride in the brougham round the countryside he stayed within the precincts of the house. When he was well enough he had his accountant, solicitor and bank manager to number 7 in order to assess as clearly as possible how he stood financially. His losses, though heavy, could have been worse, he was informed. If he sold the Seagrave establishment, he should have, with all the debts paid, enough to live on in reasonable comfort at Mooncarn. The reason for such a decline in the family fortune was shown clearly to be due more to lost contracts than to sums drawn out by Challoner, although if he wished, he was told, he could prosecute. This was not advised in view of the difficulties entailed in proving the case, and even if Clinton won, expenses could be heavy. On top of which the captain was now abroad, and no-one knew where.

'Leave it,' William said heavily and firmly when he had the position clear. 'I'll sell this house, if I have to. But give me a month or so to think over it. I must have time. Maybe a breather in sea air will blow the cobwebs away. Eh?' He tried to smile, a pathetic gesture which was embarrassing to the three advisers.

'Of course, Mr Clinton, sir,' his solicitor agreed, warmly backed by the other two. 'Meantime you have a bunch of bonds that would sell now at quite a considerable profit. It might be advisable to sell those to cover any outstanding expenses.'

William waved a hand in dismissal of further argument. 'Go ahead. You know the position. Just keep me informed.'

And so up to that point things were brought into some sort of focus, and the following week the family left for Mooncarn.

The first week passed without incident. Lise was moody, complaining that there was no youthful company there, and that she didn't see why Miss Perrot always had to follow her around.

'No one follows Priscilla,' she said to her father. 'And I am after sixteen, am I not? Then why do I have to have — what do you call it — a watch dog?'

'Because you're so pretty,' William answered. 'All pretty things have to be cared for.'

She was silent for a moment, then she said, 'You can't see me now, can you, papa?'

'I can see with my head,' William answered sharply, 'and when my head tells me to then I shall see again with my eyes. And don't ask me to explain, my dear, because I'm in no mood to answer questions.'

'Sorry, papa,' she answered in a trembling voice which indicated she was on the verge of tears. He was annoyed with himself for having upset her, and was just going to try and make amends when they were interrupted by Miss Perrot herself, who suggested they take a quick walk across the moors in the direction of Wynk.'

'If I had a horse, like Priscilla, I could ride,' Lise said. 'Why can't I have a horse?'

'One day, perhaps,' William said, 'when we can afford it. Just now we have to be careful with money.'

'Why? I thought you had lots and lots.'

'*Lise!*' Miss Perrot said quite irritably. 'Don't worry your papa when you know very well he has been ill. Come along, my dear. *Please*.'

Lise shrugged. Her dark eyes were narrowed above her sulky lips. 'Oh, all right.'

The afternoon air was fresh and invigorating. There was no wind; the short moorland turf and crisp undergrowth were silvered by a thin frosty mist that gave delicate subtle radiance to humped stones, twisted trees, and looming crest of the ancient carn far above. As the governess and girl rounded the bend from where Wynk was visible, a figure lurched towards them from behind a standing stone. He stood in the centre of the path, smiling foolishly under his woolly pointed cap.

'Goin' far?' he said, with the smile turning to a leer. 'That way be for th' piskies. Like for the piskies to get 'en then? See that theer stone thing, tes a ghostie when moon's up. Abel's seen et. Abel knaws, an' if you do come on a mooney night Abel 'll show thee. Oh, ais – like before. Remember, do ee? All pale thee was in th' dimsy night – ais, ais.' He nodded his large head, drooling slightly. 'Abel 'members.'

Lise clutched Miss Perrot's arm. 'Go away,' she cried. 'You nasty thing, you.'

The grin faded from the halfwit's face leaving the heavy lips down-turned, the small eyes mere pinpoints under the frowning brows. Miss Perrot raised the handbag she always carried and swung it before his face. 'Please move out of the way,' she said, trying to keep her voice calm. 'We are not at all afraid of piskies.'

'But o' me, y'are, eh? Strong I am. Abel's *strong*.'

He moved a further step forward. Lise would have turned and fled, but Miss Perrot, knowing that such a gesture might easily inflame the poor creature to action, held her ground, and it was at that moment that Susannah, the widow woman, Abel's old mother, appeared with a basket of mushrooms in her hand. She wore a black shawl over her head and round her shoulders, and could herself have been a figure of legend brought to life from oldest Celtic Cornwall. Her voice was hard and commanding as she cried harshly, 'Come here, Abel. What did I say 'bout talkin' to the ladies, eh? Didn't I tell thee ef you dared do et, I'd tek a stick to thy back? Well then!' She lunged at him, pulled him by one ear towards her, and boxed his ear smartly. He cowered down, dribbling. 'I wouldn'a harmed em,' he blubbered. 'I knowed that one—' He lifted an arm pointing at Lise. 'She did come all white'n shinin' once when th' auld moon called. Ais. Nuthen on, she hadn', not a shred. I do tell ee true—'

Susannah glanced shrewdly at Lise. 'What's he talkin' about, miss?' she asked. 'A fairy tale, es it? Abel doesn' generally lie –

104

not to me. Still, it must've bin someone else. Yes—' she nodded unbelievingly. 'I expect that was et. Sometimes young girls come to bathe in that old pool over theer. They shouldn'. Not far on th'other side there's a patch of black bog, a real devilish sucker it be – a death trap. Don't you go *near*, Abel, I've said, Not if you do value your life. I'm *always* telling him.' She paused, then continued, 'Well. You'll be wantin' to be continuin' your walk. Come along, Abel, and doan' ever let me catch you talkin' to ladies agen, or you'll smart for et.'

With a nod from the old woman, and a baleful glance from her son, the couple passed on in an opposite direction over the moor.

'I think we'll be going back,' Miss Perrot said stiffly. 'I didn't like the way that – that *creature* looked at you. Has he ever encountered you before, on your own?'

Lise shook her head, and laughed lightly. 'I am a young lady, am I not? And beautiful. Yes, I am beautiful, because papa said so. So why would I – what you say – converse with such an ugly one? Hah?'

'It's time you began to think less of your looks, Lise,' Miss Perrot said, 'and absorbed a little more learning. You are almost grown up now, and no doubt when you are your sister's age you will be thinking of marriage, so—'

'To a prince or a duke, perhaps,' Lise said. 'Someone who will adore me. Yes, and kiss the hem of my gown. Someone—'

'Oh, come along,' the governess said, quite irritably. 'Really! you sound quite absurd sometimes.'

Lise's lips became set in a mute stubborn line. Strange wild thoughts were stirring in her, feelings she couldn't understand herself. But one day she would, oh yes, she would, she determined. No-one was going to keep her a child forever.

*

While Lise and Miss Perrot were walking, Priscilla was in her bedroom concocting a letter to Edward Blakey:

Dear Mr. Blakey You will forgive me I hope for bothering you, and probably wasting your time, but I am wondering if you are interested in publishing poetry? I have quite a collection here, which I think are considerably more adult that the story of "Sir Robert Tyzackass" — do you remember? The childish novel I sent to you years ago when I was very young? I called myself "Cornelia Almond" but my real name is Priscilla Clinton — William Clinton's daughter; we met briefly at my birthday party not so long ago. Since then, as you may have heard, papa has had a stroke, and although his general health is improving, he is blind. We're living temporarily at Mooncarn, nr Wynk, and if you are interested to see any of my work — I have also written a few imaginative short stories — I'll pack them off to you. If I don't hear from you, I'll know it is no good, and perfectly understand.

> Thank you,
> Yours sincerely,
> Priscilla Clinton (Cornelia Almond)

She posted the letter herself the following day, saying nothing to anyone about it, not even her father. It then became a period of waiting, for post to London could take quite a long time getting through.

In the meantime, other things happened which temporarily swept all thought of publishers and books aside.

During that same week Jason appeared unexpectedly for a short hour, before setting sail again with a cargo for the Americas, as captain of one of his own ships, *The Silver King*, worked by both sail and steam.

He saw William for half an hour, after which he walked with Priscilla to a sheltered place on the moor where they could talk. When he'd kissed her and drawn her to him, they sat for a minute close and warm against each other, despite the sharp air, just content to be together, her head against his shoulder, with a late autumn wind stirring through her hair. The tall bracken was brown about them, thick and crackling from need of rain, but a sweet bed for lovers. And he loved her — oh, God, he did. After the brief silence, she glanced up at him, her eyes wide and mysterious, innocent of coquetry, yet holding such a wealth of longing that any resolve he'd had, or determination to leave her untouched and virginal until the time they could be wed, dissolved and was forgotten. His lips on hers were urgent and possessive, yet subtle, strong, drawing it seemed the very life from her body.

He laid her down, stroked the soft strands of tawny hair from her wide forehead, staring wonderingly upon this infinitely beautiful woman whom he knew was his — and his alone. Then he raised her slightly, one arm beneath her body, with the other loosening the bodice of her gown and the constricting hooks of her petticoats and skirts. His lips travelled from the firm column of her throat, over the cream soft swelling of breasts, and through to her most secret place, and rested there for a brief spell of time that was meaningless, because time itself had no sense or identity. And through the act of taking and giving that followed, there was no word or sound — not even the faintest moan from her. What pain there was, was exquisite, and precious to her — an emblem of trust unsullied by a shadow of doubt or questioning morality.

Afterwards they lay at peace for a short while with the soft whispering of nature about them. Then, regretfully, Jason got to his feet, tidied himself with a show of respectability, and said, 'Darling — it's hell to me, but I have to leave you. Only for a fortnight, though, a month at the very most—'

She got up. 'A *month*, Jason?'

'It has to be, love. We leave at six, and by rights I should be in Plynport now. But it'll pass. Something of you—' and he tapped his chest, 'will be with me every inch of the way over that damned Atlantic, and when I get back I'll have you at the altar before you can say "Jiminy"—' He forced a smile. 'Don't look so sad, my darling, my love. Just — tell me you care. I *know* you do, but *tell* me. Let them all hear — those old stones, the noisy gulls squawking, the moors, the carn. Go on, say it — say "I love Jason, and he loves me." That's a vow. Swear it — go on—'

Looking upwards at the sky which was fading now to misted grey, she swore, with her long hair loose and flying. Hand in hand then, they wandered towards the high lane bordering the moor above Mooncarn, where his horse was tethered. Minutes

later she was watching his silhouetted figure cantering westwards until at last it became a mere dot of shadow disappearing
round a bend of the track.

*

Priscilla realised that Jason had said no word concerning their love
for each other to William, or he would certainly have mentioned
the fact. He merely remarked at dinner, 'A nice young chap —
Edward's brother. Said that before, haven't I? A real adventurer,
though. Whether he'll ever make a fortune or not's debatable.
Too much of a dreamer, or visionary, if you like, I'd say.'

'Money isn't everything,' Priscilla remarked.

'No. But it counts,' her father replied. 'By the way, I've heard
young Alex is likely to arrive any day. Got a letter here. Meant to
tell you before.'

'Oh?'

'Well, can't you say any more than that? I thought you two
got on—'

'Yes, but — but do we *want* visitors just at this time, papa?
You're supposed to be resting, and—'

'Rest? Balderdash! Besides—' he gave a little chuckle, 'reckon
it isn't *me* he's coming to see, sweetheart — and you must know
that very well.'

'Papa—' She was on the verge of letting out the truth by
saying, 'don't try and make a match of Alex and I, because I
love Jason, and there'll never be anyone else — *never*'.

But she refrained in time, and was pleased she had, for a
moment later William went on, 'Well, what were you going to
say? Something about Alex?'

'No. I—'

'Shy are you? Frightened of committing yourself? Don't be,
there's plenty of time. The young man's love-sick, that's obvious.
And I'm not saying a match in that quarter wouldn't be agree-
able, a damn good help to me just now, as things are. But all the
same, love, your happiness comes first, and in time, maybe—'

'When your eyes are better,' Priscilla heard herself saying
automatically. 'Until then, papa, don't let's talk about — about
marriage and things like that. *Please*.'

Something desperate in her voice penetrated his senses. 'Oh — very well, my dear.' He reached out a hand, and she placed one of hers where he could lay his on it. It saddened her that she couldn't suddenly run to him breathlessly in happiness and excitement telling him she'd already found her love, the one man in the world she wanted to marry. But she feared to, just then, unable to face casting him down, and seeing the disappointment on his face when he heard it wasn't Alex Stern.

It must wait, Priscilla decided firmly. He already had so much to contend with apart from his blindness — loss of faith in a man he'd trusted, his abandonment by the wife to whom he'd given so much, and the possibility of facing bankruptcy, even now, if luck took another bad turn against him. But it *mustn't*, she told herself, it *wouldn't* — no, surely not. Another serious shock might kill him. If only there was something *she* could do to help — something other than marrying Alex. Why was it that the Sterns could have so much money, millions, without having to work and with no worry in the world, when her father, who was a genius and a great man, could be let down so disastrously, and partly through his own generosity? It wasn't fair.

If she'd persevered more with her writing and made a name like Currer and Ellis Bell, maybe she could have at least eased his financial stress a little. But she'd heard that even Currer Bell, whose book was more popular than Ellis's *Wuthering Heights*, hadn't really made a fortune from *Jane Eyre*. So it was useless having impossible dreams about publishing. She had to be patient, something quite alien to the independent fiery side of her nature, and do her best somehow to appear calm and responsible during Jason's absence, so that her father would feel, whatever happened in the future, he could always rely on her to understand, and give what help and support she could. Life really *was* rather like a book, she told herself. An unfolding picture in words that had a pattern to it. Every day was different. You could never quite tell what lay round the corner. Perhaps it was as well. To know what was coming might be wonderful, but it could be just the opposite.

As it happened, during the following week at Mooncarn, something occurred that proved how correct her philosophising had been.

5

The night was warm for the time of year, with eerie moonlight shadowed by mist streaking fitfully over the moor. No wind stirred the undergrowth or branches of the stunted trees — only a mere whisper of air when some small secret night creature nosed through bracken and furze. The tall stones stood bleak and cold against the hill; the pool, black and shining was rimmed by silver at brief intervals as the mist cleared momentarily, then took it once again into gathering darkness.

Lise stood at her bedroom window watching, and waiting; waiting for the house to sleep, so she could be herself — driven by a deep compelling instinct stronger by far than any reasoning she had, beyond logic of all human understanding.

It was after the old clock on the landing had struck two, that she tiptoed along the landing wearing only her nightshift and slippers, and crept downstairs, making her way down the hall to the door leading on to the moor.

When she reached the path winding below the high lane towards the forbidden territory, she stood for a moment, white through the greenish-white of cloud and air — a phantom rather than flesh and blood. Then slowly, her hands went to her head, where they quivered like the wings of some night bird about to take flight. Swaying with a curious, rhythmic reaction holding the eroticism of old gods reborn, she started to dance, slowly at first, then quicker and quicker, until she became a white flame darting in and out of the shade, brighter than the half-hidden moon, with her streaming silver hair — a will-o'-the-wisp of the elements, unconscious of danger, impelled only by the wild, unknown impulse that possessed her, driving her even closer to the glassy pool and its treacherous domain.

From the lane above, Abel, on one of his night strolls, watched. A cry like that of some terrified animal left his lips, but still she danced, at one with the elements and hidden hunger of her own savage secret joy.

Again the scream — more of a howl, left Abel's lips, and it was then that another sound pierced the air — that of cart wheels and donkey's hooves.

Tommy Treves had had a long day, and was looking for a resting place till the dawn hour. He pulled the old animal to a halt, climbed from the cart and joined Abel who was still watching motionless, mouth agape, small eyes scared like those of a rabbit in his pale round face.

He turned then, feeling Abel's hand on his shoulder.

'What's up? What's that there?' Tommy asked. 'A ghostie? Or some looney maid? What you know of et, Abel? C'mon now. Tell old Tommy. Tommy's your friend, lad.'

Abel shook his large head and his whole body shuddered. He lifted a finger as the cloud of white-gold hair in the distance bobbed in the quivering lemon light, dancing, dancing, here, there, up and down, until suddenly it stopped, and seemed to recede slowly, earthwards.

'The moon be tumblin',' Abel muttered in thick doom-like tones. 'The moon be gone soon — swallowed, swallowed. Watch et, listen. Tes the moon screamin'—' He put both great hands to his ears, and the tears were streaming down his face.

Tommy stared.

Horror gripped him. The poor half-wit was right. Only it wasn't the moon, it was some lily-white maid taken by the ugly bog-devil, and there wasn't a thing to be done about it. He turned away and got into his cart. 'C'mon, Abel, we're going together, you'n me. I've a notion who tis in that hell hole, an' we'm got to tell em at the big house — both of us, together.'

Abel pulled away. 'No. I'm not goin', not anywhere's. I'm frit o' them. My ma says—'

'Your ma edn of no account. What we've seed jus' now, we've seed, an' there won't be no wrong tales 'bout us ef we do spik

111

straight out and be honest. Ais, that's it. Honest — explain how t'was you an' me together seed a maid go under.'

Something about the little man — the set of his jutting chin and compelling gleam of the bright beady eyes under the pointed woollen cap, compelled Abel to comply. He followed him into Tommy's cart looking like some grotesque automatic dummy, and in a minute, with a jerk of the reins, and rattling of pots, pans and conglomeration of secondhand goods and the creak of wheels the odd couple were moving in the direction of Mooncarn.

In spite of his blindness, William was the first to get downstairs when the household was roused by the sound of Tommy Treves' thunderous knocking and banging at the door. His man steward was next, followed by Priscilla, without a wrap, but in a long frilled nightshift, with her hair in two thick pigtails down her back. Miss Perrot was the last of the household to arrive, having covered herself by a thick woolly cape for 'decency's sake'.

All stood behind William, as Tommy, with no attempt to soften the shock, explained their interruption at such an hour.

'There be a maid gone drownded in the bog, maister,' he said. 'We seed en, from th' top lane, Abel an' me, Tommy Treves. Twarn no ord'nary maid, surr— all whitey gold she was, an' dancin' there like a real l'il ghostie chile. We called en — Abel called—'

'The moon et wus—' Abel interrupted. 'The moon maid fallen. We seed en — *both* of us, an' that ole bog-devil — t'was waitin', just like my ma said—'

Miss Perrot gave a little scream and put her hand to her mouth, 'No? *No?* It *can't* be,' she gasped. 'Not *Lise!*'

All colour left William's face. '*Lise?* What do you mean? Isn't she in bed? Go and see, woman. Hurry up. Don't just stand there.'

Miss Perrot fled. When she returned terror was written all over her. 'She isn't there. Her wrap's on the chair and her clothes, but her slippers have gone. There's no sign of her though, except for the door — it's open a bit. And there's her bracelet — the one you gave her, sir — lying on the landing as though it had slipped off. And that side door's unlocked — the one leading to the moor—'

William gave a groan. 'Oh, my God, why was she in a room of her own? Why the devil did I allow it?' His blind eyes were turned upwards, tortured, as though seeking an answer from the heavens that would never come.

One fist was raised, clenched so tightly his arm shook. Priscilla was frightened for him. 'Papa, please don't. Don't blame yourself. She couldn't be watched *all* the time. She did it before once when she was younger, years ago, went out with nothing on. I saw her and brought her back. If it *is* Lise — and we don't know, do we? — but if it is, something would have happened sooner or later. And you *know* it would. She was different to us. There was something not — right — about her, papa. Now please *do* calm down and rest. We'll *try* to—'

'Rest?' His voice came loud in a spurt of energy. 'Don't be stupid, girl — sorry, love, didn't mean that. But we've got to get a search going — and someone must go to Wynk to inform the authorities there.' He turned to his man, 'See that's done directly. Meanwhile, have the whole house searched to make sure it isn't some monstrous trick being played on us. She had strange ideas sometimes that girl did—'

He broke off, to sip the brandy forced on him by Priscilla. A little colour returned to his face. He grasped his stick, and made his way independently to the hall chair, where he sat for moments with his head in his hands. Presently he looked up and managed to say calmly, 'Someone take those two—' pointing to Tommy and Abel '—to the kitchen. See they have something to eat and drink for their trouble. I'm grateful to them.'

Slowly life with a mechanical sort of purpose to it returned to the house.

Everything that could be done, practically, was got into action.

But at heart, both William and Priscilla realised instinctively it would be to no avail. Lise, the beautiful and unwanted child of a random union, was gone and would never return. On nights in the future when the moon was full or clouded by silvered mist, legend might have it that her spirit still danced, and was to be glimpsed at certain hours — a windblown wraith of light slipping between shadows of furze and stones over the moor. But all that was left of her lay beneath the sucking, fathomless darkness of the hungry, sucking bog.

Later William was to have that certain patch of land thoroughly drained and made as safe as possible by the best engineer and contractor available. Nothing of Lise was found but a few ethereal-looking white bones, and a pendant engraved with her initials.

During the month following her disappearance, William and his daughter left the house for good, and returned to Seagrave Square.

'It can be sold,' William said, 'if anyone wants to buy it; in that way it will help pay off a mite of what I owe.'

But by then buyers had become wary of purchasing property on land that was considered by many potentially dangerous. So William's financial problems continued, and Priscilla, sick at heart, began to review the alternative, which was in her hands only.

Perhaps if Jason had appeared within the month he'd promised her ultimate decision could have been reversed. But he didn't. His last letter, though warm and loving as ever, informed her that he was unavoidably kept abroad for a time. Following his successful trip to America, he was going to Australia, concerned with important business. But he loved and wanted her more than ever, and when he returned—

'When? *When*,' she'd thought despairingly, putting the letter aside momentarily, having only half read it. What use were words when his presence, his support — his guidance and help, were so desperately needed now?

Day by day her father was growing increasingly tense. She knew he had bad nights frequently when he brooded not only on his own sorry business plight, but on Lise's terrible end.

So it was, that after much pestering, and constant gifts and reassurances from Alex Stern that if she married him William could be on his feet in no time, and that he'd do his devilish best to make her happy, Priscilla gave in, and told her persistent suitor she would be his wife.

This was, of course, what William had hoped would happen, although when he first heard the news, conscience impelled him to ask her if she was sure.

'Sure of what, papa?' Priscilla had queried in high, bright tones, that an astute observer might have thought were almost *too* bright to be genuine.

'About Alex. That he's the one you want. A while ago when young Jason was around, I rather thought you liked him.'

There was a perceptible pause before Priscilla said, 'Yes, I *did* like him. But — it wouldn't have worked, would it?'

'Why not?' Although he dreaded the answer something deep down in Clinton — his intrepid honesty and love for his child — tore the question from him.

'Because he's the adventurous type — always away,' Priscilla answered in cool, level tones. 'Business — the shipping line and making it pay — oh, and all the other interests he has — things that crop up all of a sudden making him alter plans at the last moment — he'll always be like that, papa. Marriage to Jason would have been rather uncertain, don't you think?'

'Keeping it going in the way *you're* used to, yes,' William agreed. 'And certainly you'll have no money troubles with Alex.' He nearly added, 'Neither shall I' but wisely withheld the remark.

In the past he'd tried to influence Priscilla in Alex's favour. Now the crucial point had come he sheered away from appearing too anxious for a union where the money bags were.

And so the matter was left then and everything was arranged.

Lord Stern set wheels in motion for salvaging Clinton from bankruptcy, and contrived valuable contacts to pave the way for refiring the flame of genius in William's mind.

'You don't have to *see* plans on paper, do you?' Stern questioned one day when the two men were in conference discussing the future. 'A man of vision like you had to build things in the brain first — that's right, isn't it? I've an idea for instance — only an idea yet, mind, for donating a new theatre in Plynport. My God, isn't it needed? But hang me if I've any picture of how it should look. *You* though — I bet my bottom dollar you could soon come up with a real winner. That's so, aint't it?'

William lifted his head, and for a moment it was as though sight registered. The dark eyes burned. A spark of life seemed to quiver within as both hands closed hard on the arms of his chair.

Then he said, 'I could *try*. But getting any plan down correctly would be a teaser.'

'Not with your imagination and experience. I'd see you had the right staff to handle things, and you know you could trust me. Come on now, think on it. Your mind must be a bloody yardstick, man. Make it work; get going again. You're not done yet, not by a long chalk.'

And from that moment William Clinton began to live again.

*

Alex and Priscilla were married at Plynport Cathedral when she was nineteen and her husband seven years older. At the wishes of Lord and Lady Stern, the event was a grand affair. Priscilla wore an ivory satin gown studded with pearls in the newest style with oval hoops under her crinoline, and immense train held by two young relatives of Lord Stern's family. She had six attendants all carrying cream roses and lilies. The bride's bouquet, as befitting the wealth and status of the groom's family, was of palest pink rare orchids mingled with maidenhair fern. On her shining hair she wore a circlet of diamonds intertwined with orange blossom, from which her veil, yards long, floated ethereal as a giant butterfly's wings.

She looked beautiful, of course, and William felt a thrill of pride as he escorted her to the altar. There was no hesitancy in his step — the scene had been re-enacted several times. But he could sense her faint trembling, and hoped it was from excitement only, and that she was not uncertain or afraid. Why should she be? She had everything before her — the future was one of wealth and promise, and God willing, one day he might be granted the miracle of sight again and live to see his grand-children about him.

The cathedral, naturally, was crowded, and later, as the newly married couple drove away to the reception at Stonewell Manor, the Stern's country estate on the border of Cornwall, the street was lined with excited crowds throwing showers of rice and confetti.

There was a moment when Priscilla had a claustrophobic urge to jump out of the phaeton and run and run — rush away to somewhere quiet on a lonely shore where she could fling herself down on the damp sand, with the sea breaking gently nearby and fall asleep, waking up after her exhaustion was spent, to find it was all a dream — she hadn't married Alex at all. She was still free — a girl waiting for Jason.

The feeling was only momentary. She steeled herself to face the present and smile automatically when Alex's hand, after pressing hers, strayed to her waist possessively.

'You look *lovely*,' she heard him say, and glancing down at her ring, 'My wife. Mrs Alex Stern. Happy, are you?'

She nodded. 'Just a bit — oh, it's all been so strange — the crowds, and the incense — all those faces. I do wish—'

'What do you wish? Say it, and you'll have it.'

She managed a soft laugh.

'Oh, I'm being silly. Take no notice of me. I didn't sleep very well last night. I expect I was too excited.'

'Well — you wait till *tonight*,' Alex said meaningfully. 'We'll be alone then, my love.'

'Your love?' The words were out before she knew it.

'Well, I damn well hope so. I'll have to show you, won't I?'

And he did.

They stayed the first night at the Manor before setting off to the Continent for the honeymoon. The best suite in the stately mansion had been allotted to them, and there were flowers everywhere — on side tables, the elegant French dressing table and in crystal vases glittering from the white marble surround up the vast fireplace where logs glowed. Soon they would droop and fade from the heat. Soon, Priscilla thought, with a lurch of the stomach, the light from the chandelier would be extinguished, leaving the room in comparative darkness. But the cloying sickly-sweet scent of the drying blossoms would remain, and divested of her gown and protective underwear she would be alone — with Alex, at his mercy. She was now his wife. He had married her, it was her duty therefore to comply with any demands he made.

Duty!

For a fleeting second she closed her eyes, and tried to imagine Jason in his place. But she couldn't. Jason had belonged and always would — to the tangy sweetness of moors and sea and wild racing winds — her world. Oh, God! What had she done?

For a second she swayed, overcome by a fleeting wave of dizziness. Then she pulled herself together, hearing Alex say, 'Ah? come on now, buck up. It's over.' His voice was slightly thick. He handed her a glass of champagne from a bottle just uncorked with a pop.

She shook her head. 'Oh *no*. I couldn't. I've had too much already.'

'You take it,' he said, with his eyes, slightly blurred, peering into her face. 'Come on. I guess we'll both need it.'

Without further remonstrance she complied, and after that the rest was just a confused experience of being disrobed and laid on the bed with Alex's naked body on top of her. She felt no emotion, not even dislike, only a bewildered sense of the ridiculous. How stupid it was — this business of fumbling and grunting, and entwined limbs in undignified attitudes of athletic copulation.

Mercifully for her, Alex was himself too exhausted to continue the procedure for long, and presently, when everything was over, and he was snoring heavily, she got up, pulled the curtains aside, and managed to open a window without disturbing him.

The gentle rush of fresh air from the garden revived her a little. Later when she went back to bed and glanced down at his sleeping face under its ruffled hair, she thought how young he looked.

Perhaps after all life wouldn't be too bad, she told herself resolutely, with forced optimism. As friends they got on well together. Maybe she'd mostly be able to keep their union that way — a pact of friendship interspersed with the minimum show of passion.

Maybe.

But life had a contrary way of going its own independent course, regardless of human will — a truth that Priscilla was to learn with misgiving in the future.

6

During the next year William's health improved. The first exuberance of finding he could begin afresh quietened a little. Planning and building, naturally demanded a more balanced, practical and in some ways more thoughtful attitude than Stern had led him to believe; but with the help of an architect who'd assisted him before and understood his style and the manner his mind worked over a proposal, the first hurdle was passed. The new theatre which he'd rather suspected as being a sprat to catch a mackerel was temporarily laid aside, for a Public Town Centre contract commissioned by the Plynport City Council, on a site of unhygienic buildings which had already been cleared. The gardens were to be known as the Victoria Park, and were to include as well an arboretum, fountains playing, and a miniature lake which would entail considerable work and adaptation of the land, fresh sewerage and a complicated water system. There was, as well, to be a museum and hall for orchestral and cultural events. The hall itself would be known, specifically at Lord Stern's request, as the Clinton Hall. No protests were made at this – he was, after all, footing the bill – and William's brains as contractor and chief architect would be the genius behind the scheme. So plans proceeded. Extra rooms at Seagrave Square were converted for special offices, and new staff were employed for half the house to be used domestically by William, under a fresh housekeeper, a Mrs Downe. She was plain, practical, middle-aged, and highly recommended by Lady Stern for whom she had once worked temporarily for a brief period.

Priscilla was mildly downcast at the arrangement; she'd been happy in her youth at No 7, and the thought of never again being able to shut herself up in the old gazebo in complete solitude, saddened her until she recalled that anyway she would seldom be there. Her life now was with Alex — and by the autumn of the first year of marriage, she realised how restless and changeable it was going to be, with no real roots — no deep love of 'place' to sustain her.

Following the honeymoon on the Continent when she was whisked from place to place, from hotel to hotel, sightseeing until her head ached in the evenings, she had a spell with her husband in his London luxury flat — a period of theatre-going and ballet, of meetings with strange friends of his including Millais and Rossetti, dining out at the Café Royal, and being the focal point of all eyes in her expensive new outfits which somehow enhanced her unworldly complete lack of sophistry. In those early days Alex was proud of her. She was so beautiful like a flower untouched by the hot air of greenhouses or the adulation of his eccentric little world of artists and socialities.

Then there was the hunting season in Leicestershire. She hated it, and refused to ride to hounds. Alex shrugged, with an ill-grace. He was amazed, and hoped she wasn't going to be a prude.

Later, when they returned to the family estate on the out-skirts of Cornwall — one wing of which had been refurbished and allotted for their personal use, he forgot what minor grudges he had, and became for a brief time the apparently contented and happy friend she'd known before they married.

His sexual demands on her were light, which surprised her at first, since in their earliest days he'd appeared possessive in his blunt spoiled way. Later, when on the pretext of some mysteri-ous business or other he stayed away more and more in town or elsewhere, she began to wonder. To wonder, and think of other things — of her writings and Edward Blakey, the publisher, who had never replied to her last letter, or else the letter had gone to Mooncarn following the tragedy of Lise and been forgotten.

She never thought of Jason at all, except in dreams. And then those dreams were terrible. She either had to mount immense overhanging precipices to reach his dot of a figure briefly silhouetted above, before it disappeared, or climb massive mountains of immense boulders — every movement she made in dread of falling into dark evil masses of nothingness below. Sometimes the dream meant climbing countless steps — on and on until she reached him at the summit. She would put out a hand to touch him, but at the same second he would be gone again.

She would wake up restless, tired, with a headache. Eventually Alex noticed.

'What's the matter with you these days?' he enquired, annoyed more than worried because his father was so frequently nagging him about siring a son. 'You seem to have lost all the go in you. You woke me up last night shrieking in your sleep. Why? Are — are you going to have a child, Prissy? If it's that—'

'Oh, no. *No*. I'm just a bit — oh, maybe it's because we never seem to have time to relax.'

'Well!' he laughed, not entirely pleasantly. 'That doesn't sound like you at all — not the *you* I *used* to know.'

'But you didn't know me *terribly* well, did you, Alex? And I was a girl then, there was nothing to sap my energy, except Lise, and she—'

'You mean I *do*. I'm the cause of it. Thank you *very* much to comparing me with your mad sister.'

He was not only ruffled, but hurt.

In an attempt to soothe him Priscilla ran a hand through his hair and said placatingly, 'Alex, dear, I didn't mean that at all. And Lise wasn't exactly mad. But we're very different, you and I, and *your* friends aren't mine. They're very interesting, of course; I know that. Still, there are times when I need to be on my own for a while.'

'Why?'

She didn't mention her writing, knowing he certainly wouldn't have accepted it as a logical explanation, but probably as merely a 'high-falutin' excuse for evading her duties as his wife.

'Because I'm me,' she answered. 'And because I don't always feel like towns and art galleries and salons and being witty and fashionable and intellectually bright. I want to *relax*, as I said, just for a break, occasionally — somewhere quiet, like — Mooncarn.' The name fell from her lips half fearfully, because of the unspoken and unwished for vision momentarily invading her mind with a poignancy she could hardly bear, and which she knew her husband would have resented.

'Mooncarn! good grief! *That* abandoned place.'

'But it needn't be, need it? It's still up for sale. Of course, I know it would be a bit expensive getting things renewed there, but—'

'Expense? What the deuce does *that* matter, to Mrs Alex Stern? And that's who you are, remember.' He paused for a moment then said, suddenly decisive, 'All right, if you want that benighted mansion, you can have it. I'll tell pater and he'll no doubt pay out ten times what it's worth to *your* papa.'

'Thank you, Alex,' she smiled gently, and stood a little on tip-toe to kiss him.

He hardly responded. 'It's all right,' he said gruffly, 'there's nothing to thank me for.' And indeed, when he came to think about it later, he realised how true his statement had been.

Although he was fond of Priscilla and proud of her as a wife, there were increasing times lately when he had become mildly bored. A retreat where she could be happy on her own at intervals could be convenient, leaving him free to pursue a few of the off-beat pursuits and amorous little side pleasures that had been so diverting during his bachelor days.

Alex was true to his word. Mooncarn became once more a part of the Clinton heritage, being legally made over to Mrs Alex Stern, the daughter of William Clinton who had formally had the property restored and made habitable.

William himself, though gratified, was surprised at the deal, and at Priscilla's wish to retain it in the family. Memories of what had happened to Lise were still too dark and frightening to him to contemplate ever visiting the district again. The place for his daughter must represent therefore an emotion stronger than fear or grief, or any logical explanation, and he was mildly troubled that he could not define what.

Perhaps the niggling memory of Jason hovered somewhere in the background of his brain, but he refused to regard it as important. She had cared for the young fellow, yes — in her youthful exuberant way. But she was a wife now, with everything material she needed at her disposal. He could only hope it was enough, and that her wilful heart was not chasing a shadow.

In the meantime, during the stimulus of choosing what new furnishings would be required for the house, of arranging for its redecoration, and employing a gardener, and a caretaker-housekeeper — one far younger and more efficient than the widow-woman, old Susannah, Priscilla received a letter from Edward Blakey.

My dear Priscilla, I was delighted to hear from you — although I did attend your wedding, you were far too elusive a bride for me to contact at the reception. However, you would have received my congratulations to you both which I now enclose.

Dear girl, if only I'd known before that you were Cornelia Almond — I should have contacted you long ere this. When I received in the past a copy of the *Adventures of Sir Robert Tyzackass*, I had no idea of your address or true identity, and am afraid I passed over your script rather hurriedly, thinking it had been written by a lady of adult years with a certain talent but not the necessary learning (I refer to spelling chiefly) to make publishing a profitable undertaking.

Knowing now how very young you were — a mere child, I wonder if you could return a full length script of the novel — *in its original form and language* — and this is most import-ant. It *could* be that we, as a firm, might have second thoughts about the story. If I remember — well I certainly do — the narrative was amusing and stimulating and certainly extremely individual. As a book it could possibly prove to be a unique production, especially if published simultaneously with your poems.

Yes, I like your poetry. If you have more do send them along, and when they have been considered with the rest, I'll again contact you immediately.

Do remember, though, not to alter the childlike style of writing concerning the heroic Robert Tyzackass, in *any* way at all. This is important, and if you *have* done so during the passage of time, I'd be grateful for it to be changed back to the original (*plus* the amusing spelling).

   Waiting to hear from you.

Yours very sincerely,

Edward Blakey

P.S. Jason is still traversing the wilds of nowhere. When next I see or contact him, I will give him news of your marriage.

There was a long pause while Priscilla sat with the letter in her hand, staring through a window into the garden of the manor. The trees and herbage — the early roses and flowering pink cones of chestnut blossom were seen through her eyes as a mirage, and did not really register. A confusion of emotion swept through her — of excitement at Edward Blakey's proposals for her work, intermingled with a conscious sense of loss and foreboding of Jason's reaction, when he heard of her marriage. It *did* appear that her ambitions as an authoress could quite likely come to fruition at last, however modestly. But without Jason, without the fire and reality of living, the achievement for that brief interim held a bitter-sweet irony.

She would have sacrificed — oh, so willingly — any faint possibility to fame hovering on the horizon — to feel once more Jason's arms about her, his lips on her mouth. But that was over, she told herself reluctantly. Never again would she sense the thrill and leap of love turning her body to flame. Her own beauty was a mockery — useless without the one person in the world who mattered. Just for a moment she hated herself and the circumstances that had impelled her into her fruitless union — hated her father's incapacity and lack of sight — the foolishness that had driven him to marry Olivia and trust Challoner, and his obvious wish, when fate went against him, for an alliance with the Sterns. She'd sacrificed herself, she knew she had. Papa! Always papa had come first.

The next moment she was ashamed of her bitterness, knowing that her actions had not been forced on her, but had been by her own will. If only Jason had been near at the time — he hadn't kept his word though. A month he'd said — only a month he'd be away. But it had been much longer. She had no way of knowing he had indeed written to her — again after that one first letter — a letter that had somehow gone astray. So Jason, too; Jason was at fault as much as herself, perhaps even more.

Suddenly straightening her form to a stance of determination, almost rigidity, she put the letter from Edward into her reticule. She had something left after all — the purpose of which she'd first been conscious when she was a tiny girl — to write. To express all the wonderful things that were happening round her in the early years — the waking of springtime and heady tangy scents of autumn — the lilac tree shaking its petals like purple rain on a summer breeze — the unknown mystery of the future, and the delights of running and skipping and breathing the sweet air — of rolling in the hay, and listening to the sad-sweet call of the cuckoo over the fields. The adventures that lay ahead, of colourful people and gipsies, a host of fictional figures created from her imagination and somehow given life, characters to be woven into her own stories in a kind of tapestry — written down so that other people could share and enjoy them. Oh, there was richness left for her somehow, still. There had to be; because she knew she had a gift, and the gift now could be used as a force to give her existence some kind of motivation and goal.

Alex, who'd had one of his frequent spells in London returned that day, and in the bedroom later, hoping against hope that he might share a little of her enthusiasm over Edward's letter, she showed the note to him.

He looked at first surprised, then faintly amused at the epistle. His eyebrows arched, as he said, 'My! oh *my*! — didn't know we really *did* have a budding Jane Austen — or should I say Currer Bell, in the family. Good luck, old girl.' She winced, as he continued, 'Tyzackass! you've got one there!' he gave a mock bow, and winked. 'That's what comes of being Lord Stern's daughter-in-law, my girl. But don't get too cocky about it. Try and please the old boy by giving him a son. That's what *he*'s after.'

'It will happen or not,' Priscilla replied shortly, refolding the letter and putting it back in her reticule.

He didn't understand one bit, and never would, she thought.

Breeding! That was all that counted to him, horses, women and a child — or rather a boy.

Irritated she turned to leave the room, but he pulled her back and gave her a dutiful kiss. 'Cheer up,' he said. 'What's the matter? What've I done?'

'Nothing, Alex. It's just me. I feel a bit — headachy.'

'Oh, Lord! not another of those. You've had one or two lately, haven't you? You're not by any chance—'

'*Enceinte?* No, I'm not.'

'Well — don't go all moody because that publishing fellow's sucking up—'

'He isn't.' Her temper flared. 'Why do you always think the reason for anyone being interested in anything I do, and trying to help — is simply because I've married into *your* family? I could say the same of your eccentric friends in Bloomsbury — those ex-pre-Raphaelites and their hangers on. *Mostly* the hangers on.'

'Oh! I see.'

The words told her nothing.

'Well,' he resumed after a few moments had passed. 'I hope you're not going to be a bore, Priscilla. Since our marriage I *must* say you've not been exactly stimulating.'

She sighed. 'I think you've had all you wanted of me, haven't you?'

'Mmm,' he agreed. 'In a way, I suppose.'

'And you have so many others also to oblige, haven't you? I'm not blaming you. Just letting you know I'm quite aware there are — other women in your life ready to flatter you on the altar of your sexual ego.'

He threw back his head and laughed.

'You really *are* the limit, Prissy. What an elegant way of describing the situation. But how, may I enquire, did you find out?'

She faced him squarely.

'Sometimes — generally, after your absences in London and elsewhere — you have quite an odour about you.'

'*Odour?*'

'Smell, Alex, smell; scent, perfume, and certainly not mine.

There are other things too. I haven't said anything before, because—' she shrugged, 'I didn't think it was my business, not while you were discreet, but—'

'No. It damn well wasn't, and isn't.'

'Then that's all right, isn't it?' She spoke stiffly, wondering how they had come to this? Already they were arguing sordidly like any disillusioned middle-aged couple with no longer even any liking for each other. In the past, before their marriage, they had been able to laugh and have fun. Now, somehow, all that had gone. Being a Stern seemed to have taken spontaneity and light-heartedness from their union before they'd properly got to know each other. Or perhaps they *had*. Perhaps reality had struck them like a bomb. She'd known Alex was a bit of a playboy, of course – he'd had a name for it. They'd joked about his numerous fleeting affairs of which he'd been quite frank, before he'd seriously considered marriage. He'd been an amusing raconteur, and she'd taken most of his titillating amours with a pinch of salt. Now they savoured to her of bad taste, and quite unnecessary. She was his wife, legally, anyway. If he had to continue with his indulgences it was surely up to him to be subtle and not let her know.

Sensing her disapproval, Alex said, suddenly contrite, 'You know you're the only woman I care about, Prissy, or you ought to. Don't let us quarrel, love, about sidelines that mean nothing. If you enjoyed things a bit more when we met my friends – were more sociable – well, then those others wouldn't have a chance in hell.'

He looked so sincere, so solemn and suddenly young, that Priscilla managed to smile. 'All right,' she said. 'Let's forget it. I'm not a prig. At least I hope not.'

'And I'm not half such a bad boy as you seem to believe. Truth is you get me jittery sometimes.'

She stared. '*Jittery?*'

He nodded. 'You're so clever, Prissy, so upsides with everything, in spite of your innocent looks. And all that writing stuff, it makes me feel – useless at times.'

'*Useless?*'

She frowned. He took her chin between finger and thumb, nodded, kissed her full on the lips and said, 'Yes, honest. Just at the moment, mind — all that Tyzackass stuff — then at others—' a hand went round her waist slipping downwards to the small curves of buttocks and thighs '—at others I know all's fine, if I can bring you to see sense — like this.' He lifted her up and carried her to the bed, where a second or two later, without preliminaries he was claiming and taking her in his usual perfunctory practical way that left no time for the first stirring of longing to rise in her.

Nevertheless, she accepted him stoically, and managed to conceal her relief when the boring procedure was over.

Matters might have gone on in this way considerably longer than they did had not an occasion arisen at the manor when Priscilla, after departing early for a whole day in Plynport concerning certain furnishing for Mooncarn, returned three hours before the time arranged, to find Alex lying with Selina, a red-haired housemaid, in the connubial four-poster Priscilla had shared with her husband since their marriage.

Both were lying completely naked, over the silk quilt, limbs entwined in the last groaning throes of intercourse.

Hearing the creak of the door, Alex still breathless, sprang up, leaving the girl to cower down with the silk coverlet pulled over her chin. For quite half a minute there was a pause during which Priscilla stood still staring. Alex, rapidly pulling his wrap round him, blusteringly started trying to explain that for which no explanation could suffice.

'I — y'see, my love — the folks went off for the day, and — and I was kind of lonely. It wasn't Selina's fault. It just—'

'Happened, I suppose?' Priscilla's voice was cold, deadly calm. 'Yes. I understand. Like this—' she swept forward suddenly, went to the bed, pulled the quilt from the girl's quivering form, and slapped her sharply on each cheek. After that she threw a heap of clothes lying on the floor at the quivering creature, and said, 'Now, get out. And don't let me see your face in this house again. You'll leave immediately. Understand? Just pack your bag and go.' The girl jumped up and pulled an eiderdown round herself.

'I'm sorry, ma'am, I—'

'Sorry, you slut – *sorry*?'

'Here, I say, Prissy, that's enough,' Alex interjected feebly, but with an effort at being firm. 'You can't do that—'

'Can't I indeed? I think it's my prerogative to employ whom I wish in my home. And I've no fancy for trollops.'

With one hand to her face, the other clutching the covering round her, the girl fled. Alex strode to the door and shut it. Then he returned, faced Prissy, and said coldly, 'Not exactly a ladylike thing to do, was it?'

Trembling from the impact, but trying not to show it, Priscilla answered, 'No. But then perhaps I'm not a lady.'

'Evidently.'

'Neither are you a gentleman.' Anger overtook her again. 'Do you realise what *you've done*, Alex? How the servants must have sniggered behind my back? Because it's not the first time, is it? And under our own roof! Is it habitual? Tell me. I want to know.'

'Oh, don't be ridiculous. *Habitual.* I didn't want the bloody thing to happen. I'm not a fool. But you weren't here – she came in, to turn down the bed or something, and—'

'And you *happened* to be here, and conveniently jumped into it. I see.' Her expression was once more stony.

'But you *don't*, you know – *understand*. That's just it. You're so darned wrapped up in your fictitious novels and poetry you haven't a clue what makes a man like me tick—'

'Tick,' she laughed contemptuously.

'Yes. *Want* a woman, in a straightforward flesh-and-blood way. It's romance with you – *words*. Words, words, words—'

'You didn't appear to think so when you pressed me into marrying you.'

'You were different then. Unattainable. I guessed – wrongly apparently, that beneath the entrancing coy Miss Clinton was quite a passionate little piece!'

'Little *piece*! What a term.'

He shrugged. 'Well, you know what I mean. Anyway—' he frowned momentarily, '—don't try to pretend you weren't

130

ready for a bit of fun on the sly. What about your birthday affair?'

She stiffened.

'What do you mean?'

'I saw you sneak off with that publisher's brother — *ah*, yes. And you didn't come back, did you? Not for quite a time. Long enough for me to wait a bit, then take off and leave you to it. "Very well," I said to myself. "Let her have her little game. In the end I'll get her, because she wants what I've got — gold to rescue her old man, and the other'll come. We're pals," I thought, "friends. When she's my wife, I'll soon teach her the rest." But you're so high and mighty, Priscilla. So — oh hell. What does it matter—'

She sighed. 'Not to you, perhaps. But at the moment—'

'Yes, go on. At the moment?'

'I feel somehow — degraded.'

'Oh Lord! now melodrama.'

'And don't sneer. Call it what you like. But I've got to get away, Alex, have a change somewhere.'

'A holiday, you mean. All right, if you think it will help things, I'll get a few addresses — the Continent—'

'*No*,' she interrupted sharply. 'I didn't mean together. On my own. I'd like to go to Mooncarn.'

He laughed sharply, derisively, a sound something between a cough and a guffaw. '*That* benighted place, to moon and brood in secret, I suppose? Like a nun at the confessional. Very well, my dear. If that's what you want — go ahead to your virgin sanctuary. And may the ghost of your mad sister leave you in peace.'

'What a — beastly thing to say. *Cruel*.'

He turned away, remarking lightly, 'Not at all — just ordinary, Prissy. Commonplace, unlike you.'

With which barbed comment he proceeded to ignore her, and marched to the dressing room with his clothes over his arm.

So it was that by the end of the week Priscilla had set off for Cornwall.

8

Mooncarn had been sufficiently refurnished and decorated to give it a refreshingly different atmosphere — at least superficially — when Priscilla arrived. It was late afternoon as the brougham drove up the short drive, depositing her luggage and herself at the front door. The new caretaker, who was also going to act as cook-housekeeper was already waiting for her; she was a healthy, plump, clear-complexioned woman — the widowed sister of a farmer's wife from the near side of Wynk. It had been arranged that each evening she would return to the farm, as she had a young daughter there, and would be at Mooncarn by nine o'clock the following day. The staff, in all, was to comprise a general manservant, a gardener who would act as part groom with a stable boy, and a girl to live in. Priscilla intended only to use certain of the rooms, and had not wished the place to be 'cluttered by staff', as she'd put it to Alex, before making final arrangements.

Alex had shrugged and said, 'All for the simple life. Well, that's your affair. I'm afraid it wouldn't suit me.'

Looking round on her first evening, Priscilla was pleased by her own choice of furnishings. Most of the newly papered walls were in a soft light gold, giving a mellow effect of sunshine, and providing a harmonious setting for the old furniture. Lounge chairs had been re-upholstered in a peach shade, blending tastefully with brown carpeting. The dining room had not yet been completed, but Priscilla didn't mind that — it faced north and was a somewhat chilly room.

Upstairs the small bedroom overlooking the western moors stretching to Wynk had been given soft paint in misty blue, and cream paper for the walls. She had always been fond of that particular 'cubbyhole' as she called it, although it was more than that. But there was something intimate and living about it, a secret happiness that time had somehow left unsullied, and which she looked upon as her own. In the past it had been used as a sewing room, but she had also written many of her poems there, and to Priscilla it had become almost a part of herself.

Mrs Bogwaneth, the housekeeper, had arranged a tall vase of chrysanthemums in a recess on the landing. Their autumn earthy scent hovered nostalgically in the air as Priscilla walked along to the bedroom with the kindly woman, preceded by the manservant who deposited bags and other luggage at the door before opening it and touching his forelock as he departed.

The two women went in. A log fire sputtered from the grate emphasising the welcoming mellow light of the setting sun streaming through a side window.

Priscilla gave a sigh of pleasure. 'How nice it is to be back, and you've followed my directions so marvellously, Mrs Bogwaneth. It's just as I wanted—'

'I did my best, ma'am, in the time. O'course the painting in the rest of the house isn't done with yet, the decorators showed us the letter you'd sent to leave it for a bit, and there's some outside to be got through when it's convenient to you. I hope the new rugs and pieces o' furniture you ordered are put in the right places – they came by cart from Truro but the man was a careful sort and I don't think anything's harmed. You'll notice the new blue and cream curtains I've put up here – run them up myself, I did. Then, downstairs in the small lounge, I threw the dark velvet things out. Oh, the dust! – you wouldn't believe. You mayn't like the ones I've chosen, but the material seemed nice, subdued, but quite useful – heavy linen; the blue cornflower pattern against the cream had a cheering up effect, I thought. Pardon me, ma'am, if I've taken much on myself, but I did want you to feel a happiness here – specially after all that terrible business with your sister—' She broke off, an earnest expression on her broad face. 'Forgive me, Mrs Stern, ma'am, I don't want to be personal. Hope I've not spoken out of my place.'

Priscilla shook her head. 'Not at all. You've been of tremendous help. What I'd have done without your assistance in looking after things, I don't know. I'm very grateful. And please don't be afraid of referring to Lise. I'm not going to brood about it. It was a dreadful shock, of course — especially to my father—'

'Ah, yes. Poor gentleman. Is he—'

'Oh, he's *much* better, which is the main thing. He's immersed in work again, and managing wonderfully in spite of his eyes. As for me—' she broke off, shrugged, and continued in forced bright tones '—I can't complain about anything. I have all I want materially speaking, and that's what few people can say, I suppose.'

'Yes, miss, I mean ma'am.' There was a short pause before the woman continued in a more thoughtful vein, 'Everything depends on what folks do want. Some want riches, some power, some to be forever chatterin' away in crowds, others shuttin' theyselves away in some dark hole like an old mole, all different — an' that's how it should be to my way o' thinkin'. It'd be a dreary world if all of us were after the same thing.'

'Yes,' Priscilla agreed automatically, with her thoughts suddenly and unwantedly turning to Jason. 'That's true.'

'And don't you go listening to any native of these parts who makes out he's seen the ghost of a young girl walkin' the moors near the bog,' Mrs Bogwaneth resumed briskly. 'I didn't *want* to bring the subject up, but it's bound to reach your ears sooner or later — the gossip, ma'am. They're a superstitious crowd round here, but it's all just old wives' talk — stuff and nonsense. I don't believe the dead return, and never have. And if anyone goes whisperin' tales in your ears, just ignore it, ma'am.'

'I intend to,' Priscilla said crisply. 'I'm not superstitious either. I leave that to poor, simple creatures like Abel. How *is* Abel, by the way?'

'Oh. Same as ever. He's partly the reason for my speakin' out like I have. Not that there's any harm in him — never was. I'm sure he'd never hurt a fly. But he *does* have queer moments, and odd sayings that drop out just when you don't expect it. And another thing — he *will* come out on a moonlit night and stand there watchin' that old bit o' land where the bog was. It's cleared now, as you must know. But Abel's got a habit of *watchin'*, ma'am — and his old mother can do nothin' to stop him. Once I caught him at it, and said, "What are you doin' there, Abel? Your ma'll be waitin' and lookin' for you", and he said, "I waitin' for the moonmaid. Soon she'll come out o' that theer black land" — you know how he speaks — "an' we'll go a'dancin' together till the marnin' come". Yes, he said that. So — well — I've been preparin' you for what *might* happen, Mrs Stern, and I wouldn' want you to get a shock.'

Priscilla smiled reassuringly. 'I'm sure I won't, and you needn't worry. I think I understand poor Abel. He was quite infatuated by Lise.'

'All the same, ma'am, take care.'

Priscilla said nothing, but smiled reassuringly. Abel, to her, had become merely an indigenous quality of the untamed fey atmosphere of Mooncarn's surrounding territory — as much a part of the landscape as the boulders and standing stones — the giant fingers of rugged cliffs clawing into the sea, and the winding tangled paths struggling over the stretch of moors towards Wynk. The boggy patch of ground was now as safe as it ever could be, and the few fragile remains of her half-sister had been given burial in parish church land.

One afternoon, shortly after her arrival at Mooncarn, she took a stroll to the spot which stood in a slight dip of the moors inland, and served two small country parishes. It was a still, quiet autumn afternoon, and no one was about. An air of peace hovered over the ancient gravestones and one or two more modern ones of lighter granite. A small white stone had been erected near the Lychgate, just inside, on which were inscribed the words 'To the memory of Lise, daughter of William Clinton who died in 1858 aged 16 years.'

A small bunch of late wild flowers lay immediately below. Priscilla bent down and saw on a small smudged piece of cardboard a message written by an obviously untutored hand which at first meant nothing to her. Then after puzzling over the distorted letters she managed to decipher '—fromabel wivluv.'

Priscilla's heart jerked, not with pity for the lovely young girl who she felt had nothing to do with that quiet spot whose restless spirit — if any — must be elsewhere, floating and dancing by brook and fern — but for the poor simpleton whose life she obviously still haunted with memories of her exquisite pale body and elusive mass of shining hair.

Casually Priscilla bent down and laid there a spray of berries and crimson autumn leaves she'd gathered beside Abel Adam's poignant tribute. Then, determined not to brood, she got up quickly and walked away to the point just beyond the gully, from where Wynk was clearly visible. In the distance below, the cottages gleamed cream and grey along the narrow street leading down to the small harbour. A few boats rocking on the surface of the water, caught a film of gold from the fading sun which was already silvered by early rising mist.

Taking a deep sweet breath of tangy air into her lungs, Priscilla was drawn back into the past — to the day when she'd first met Jason, and he'd stopped to chat with her for a few moments, his blue eyes intent, and suddenly alert. She'd been a child then, but something had grown up in her from that very moment, and she'd sensed without properly accepting it that there'd be a time when they'd be more than friends — much, *much* more. Oh, yes. Her heart had known — had caught in one of her rare moments of precognition — a fleeting awareness of destiny beyond her control; something her youthful mind had failed temporarily to understand.

Years had passed, but here she was, back again because something had been imprinted on the locality's atmosphere that would remain forever magical to her, although she might never see Jason again. After standing motionless for some minutes, she turned and slowly made her way back to the house. The light was quickly fading, leaving the sky a misty purple shot with streaks of dying gold.

She met no one, and saw no living thing stir, except the glimmer of a gull's wing soaring to the sky, and to her left, over the moor, the slim shape of a fox streaking from the heather across the short turf of the high ridge. Yet the air and earth were pregnant with unknown life, and against her will she felt longing rise in her — the longing for comfort and a man's strong arms about her, just one man's — Jason's. For this very reason she sharpened her pace and steeled her will to the future. In the morning she must write to Edward Blakey and thank him for his letter. What a mercy she now had an escape through her work — escape from the aching business of hungering for the impossible.

Dear Mr. Blakey [she wrote] or may I call you Edward now? I was so delighted to have your letter, and know that you liked my poems. As you will see from the above address I am now at Mooncarn for a change on my own. Life in Plynport since my marriage to Alex became rather hectic and I wanted a period to think about my writing prospects, including, of course, the Tyzackass novel. I've brought the original script with me, and what I tried to change from a very childish style to more adult terms I can easily change back, and when I have a reasonable copy I will send it to you. Thank you very much for your interest.

    With best wishes
             Yours sincerely,
             Priscilla Stern (née Clinton).

She slipped the note into an envelope, addressed it, and gave it to the man to take in to Wynk from where it would be sent with other post to catch the mail coach from Plynport for London.

After that she called at the Craze farmhouse to have a word with Ned.

'So you'm be Mistress Stern now, I do hear,' he said, his ruddy face beaming to see her.

'Yes, Ned, a married woman — a matron,' Priscilla replied, letting him shake her hand warmly.

'Eh, now I doan' b'lieve that,' came the reply. 'No *matron*. You'll always be the wild lovely young girl we all do love, an' that's for sure. But you'm happy, I do hope?'

'Of course, as happy as most wives, I guess. But why do you ask?'

'I just thought as how you'm lookin' a bit — whisht, now, beggin' your pardon, Miss — ma'am. But there you've had much to worry thee, that's so, edn't et. First your poor father bein' took bad an' blind — then that sister o' yours gettin' bogged. What an end. No wonder Mr Clinton took against Mooncarn. An' his new lady-wife too! forgive me if I sound's if I'm takin' a liberty, Miss Priscilla — I mean ma'am — but I couldn't tek to her, not your stepmother in any way 't'all. Not that I had much t'do with her that one time she did come — haughty-like an' starin' down her nose as though all else were dirt. Ef you ask me he's well rid o' her. Still, on top of everythin' else it must've bin hard to tek.'

'In a way, yes. But papa's wonderfully courageous, Ned, and my father-in-law, Lord Stern, has helped him to get to work again — backed him in every way possible. I'm terribly grateful to him.'

'Ah well, they say good often follows the bad,' Ned observed, 'an' I hope all'l be good for your family from now on, Miss Priscilla.'

'Thank you.'

She left him soon after that brief chat, and on the high lane above, shortly before reaching Mooncarn, she saw Tommy Treves leading his donkey cart in the opposite direction, towards Wynk. She waved automatically, and called, 'Hullo,' with one hand making a tunnel of her voice. He turned his head, stared for a moment in Priscilla's direction, then drew the cart to a halt, jumped down, tethered the donkey to a tree stump where she could nibble the undergrowth, and hurried down the slope towards her, nimble as ever in his blue smock, with the perky woollen cap perched a little sideways over his odd coloured eyes. His greeting was effusive. He looked more than ever like a mischievous bow-legged old gnome, Priscilla thought, as he delivered a number of gossiping little tales, some of which she believed, others too fantastic to be true.

'An' there g'win' to be Autumn Fair Chygwarren way on th' downs, come Saturday,' he told her after his fund of humour and drama were exhausted, 'Will thee be g'win', Missus Priscilla?'

'A fair?' She felt a stab of excitement. 'I'd love to, but it's rather a way to walk, and the only horse in the stables now is Rom, used for the gardener and lad — Merlinda was sold when papa was in need of capital—'

'Oh, don't thee worry 'bout transport, maiden,' Tommy said with a wicked grin and a wink. 'Jessie there'll carry thee,' he cocked his thumb towards the donkey. 'Give me a chance to stretch these crooked ole legs o' mine for a bit.'

'*Poor* Jessie.'

'Not at all. She'm in good form. Live longer'n me I shudn' wonder, or mebbe we'll tek off together one day an' give ole Gabriel a problem at the Golden Gate. "Why wat's this then?" he'll say, scratchin' his yeller halo. 'A *donkey*? We doan gen'rally kip pastures bright for such long-eared ones as he". "He's a *her*, surr," I'll be tellin' him, "an' ef you won't accept Jessie, then down we goes to th' other place where virtue edn' measured by ears or lack of 'em".'

Priscilla laughed. 'Tommy, you're really wicked sometimes.'

'Ah, yes. An' that's what kips me hale an' hearty, ma'am. No room for misery makers, I haven'. Psalm singin' weren't near to my likin' — nor never will be.' He paused, then added, 'Must be gettin' goin' now. What about Saturday, then? Two o'clock up there, in the lane? I'll be stayin' an hour mebbe at Chygwarren, then back same way — have to reach Zaren 'fore sun sets, so you wouldn' have no worries 'bout bein' late home.'

Priscilla agreed to the arrangement, and found herself childishly elated at the prospect ahead.

When the day arrived Tommy was in the lane waiting for her at the time arranged. She was wearing a dark cloak, over a crimson skirt and bodice trimmed with black braid, and a small bonnet-shaped hat tied under the chin with lacy veiling to keep it secure from the high wind blowing.

Tommy led the old donkey leaving Priscilla sitting like a young gipsy queen on the front seat; with the pots, pans and other wares rattling behind her.

The fair, held in a flat fold of the downs, inland, was in full swing when they arrived. There were side shows, including a

139

Punch-and-Judy show, a fortune teller in her tent, gingerbread stalls, a juggler balancing balls on his nose, dancing bear, a wrestling booth, and a crowd of natives from surrounding parts dancing to a merry tune of a fiddler. The crowd of sightseers, including tinners, merchants, and a few gentry, was quite large. Spirits were high, and there was considerable bargaining for the purchase of cattle on display and for a woman put up for sale by her husband. The woman in question was large, black-haired and plain, but she looked strong and healthy, and was being widely acclaimed by her buccolic heavy-browed spouse, for her cooking and household ability.

Priscilla, shocked rather than amused, found herself on the scene when the woman, after being prodded and pushed, was finally sold, with a knock of the hammer, to the highest bidder.

A figure stepped forward, tall, fair-haired, in seaman's attire, who, after paying, led her away on one arm. In a kind of trance Priscilla followed, and caught up with the couple as the stranger delivered his human merchandise to a comrade — or maybe servant, standing on the fringe of the merry-making. 'Take her to the kiddleywink near Wynk,' she heard the man say. 'I'll be along presently. See she has drink and a meal, and find her a comfortable pair of boots, for God's sake.'

He turned to make his way back into the jostling throng, and then two pairs of eyes — met — Jason's and Priscilla's.

She stood rigid, hardly able to accept what she'd just witnessed, yet aware that it was true. Her chin lifted defiantly, there was a cold set of determination on her lips. But behind the fire of her luminous eyes, misery, hatred, and longing, were curiously intermingled.

'*You!*' she said at last, in low vibrant tones. 'You *bought* her, a *woman.*'

His mouth, too, was grim.

'I can explain.'

'Of course you can. It's a very convenient habit of yours, I'm sure.'

He put out a hand to touch her, but she shuddered and drew away as if contaminated.

140

'Leave me alone. Don't touch me.'

'Dear, dear! I'm so sorry I offered. These – this attire of mine may not appear particularly cultural. But I happen to *work*, Mrs *Stern*.'

She winced.

'Oh, yes, I've learned of your marriage,' he continued, striving to keep his temper under control. 'I was surprised, I must admit. I rather thought we had a contract—'

'*You* thought.'

'Apparently I was deceived.'

'You? But—'

Suddenly he grabbed her arm, and without more ado pulled her after him some way towards the ruined remains of an old Count House where they could be safely private and hidden from the crowd.

There, breathless and gasping, with her bonnet hanging loose behind her shoulders, and her tawny hair fallen from its combs, she lifted a hand and struck him across the face. He gritted his teeth. 'Any more of that,' he said, 'and I'll put you over my knee and give you the spanking of a lifetime. And believe me, Priscilla, I *mean* it.'

One hard look at the set of his face warned her that he really did.

She set her lips mutinously. 'How *dare* you drag me along like any – any—' she broke off, lost for words.

'Because I love you,' he interrupted bluntly. 'You too – after what we'd had together, that last time – I believed you felt the same. Why? – *Why* on earth did you do it?'

'What?'

'Marry that dilettante, of course. What else?'

She stared at him a moment or two, before answering. Then she remembered dully, 'A month you said. A month at the most, and you'd be back. Instead you went to Australia. You never wrote from there, and instead of *one* month it was two – three, more – oh, such a long time. My father was ill, then he went blind. Lord Stern was very kind, and Alex wanted to marry me. It seemed the only thing to do – at the time, because—'

'Because he was rich.'

The contempt did not escape her. 'Yes — *yes*,' she cried wildly. 'Papa was ill and in financial difficulties. So—'

'You sold yourself. He *bought* you.'

'Quite. Like *you* bought that woman at the sale just now. Only not so blatantly, because Alex and I were friends. We got on together at the time.'

'And now?'

She looked away, not wishing him to see the quiver of her lips. 'Does it matter? It's done. I'm married.'

'It matters,' he said. He turned her round to face him, and for the first time she noticed the hurt, the deep pain in his eyes. 'It all seemed so *right* — you and I,' he continued. 'I didn't think anything could come between.'

'But then — neither of us knew about my father. If you'd been there, perhaps—' She hesitated, adding in a rush of words, 'But no. There wasn't anything else I could do. If *you'd* seen someone you loved suddenly helpless and losing everything — in a dark world! so helpless, Jason. It was terrible.'

'*That* I can understand. But not the final act. He'd had success and made a name. Perhaps if he'd attended more to his domestic affairs, and less to his great schemes that last marriage of his wouldn't have ended as it did. Then Lise—'

'Don't criticise my father,' she flared.

'Why not? *You're* criticising *me*, trying to make me the scapegoat, but we're all masters of our own actions, or should be. Lise didn't appear from under a gooseberry bush. Your father, I've no doubt, had quite a lot of pleasure in her begetting. So don't go all sentimental about him and try and make him the suffering saint. He wasn't one — just a fine man with a number of human weaknesses that landed him in a mess. The point is — you sacrificed your own happiness — and mine incidentally — to feel good, and all square with your conscience.'

'How *can* you say such a thing?'

'It's true. He'd have got through, somehow, and you know it, deep down. As for the Australian business — I did write to you once. Did you not get the letter? Then it was all such a rush—'

'What was?'

'The chance of a lifetime, of running the Blakey Shipping Line between the Colony and Britain for the exportation of wool, mainly, and coal. It meant money, Priscilla, and security I thought, for *us*. A contract was given me — ironically — by your new father-in-law, Lord Stern and I went out all hell for it. It means a larger ship, of course, maybe two. But Stern himself seems prepared to back it—' he broke off, shaking his head slowly. 'He meant well, the old boy, I don't doubt it. So I clinched the deal in the right quarters and when I came back I thought — well, it's of no account now. I wasn't to know, was I, that in the meantime the one woman I ever loved or was ever likely to, had jumped into holy matrimony with his noble lily-livered son. As for that sale just now — she's a good cook apparently, and I've hired the woman for a ship's kitchen—'

With sobs tearing at her throat, but remaining dry eyed, Priscilla repeated several times over, 'You should have told me — let me know. You should have—'

'I should've collected you and carried you off, before you did such a damned hypocritical thing,' Jason interrupted. He held her at arm's length again for a moment or two, searching her face closely, before continuing in harder tones, 'Unless, of course, I was fooled. Did the prospect of becoming Lady Stern one day, I wonder, prove eventually to be more to your taste than that of becoming the wife of an ordinary sea captain with no handle to his name?'

Priscilla pulled herself away with a strength and violence he'd not expected. Then she cried furiously, 'For that I despise and detest you, Jason Blakey. Go away — leave me, I hate you — oh, how I *hate* you—'

She turned and rushed from him, cape and hair flying, back into the crowd, before he could remonstrate further. Whether he followed or not she didn't know, or care at that moment. Emotions of loss and terrible unhappiness, blurred all sense of reason in her. All she wanted was to be away where she could give vent to her distress on her own, with the painful knowledge that indeed everything was over finally now between herself and

Jason. He would probably never wish to speak to her again and the feeling was mutual.

She found Tommy Treves at the opposite far end of the fairground, auctioning his wares, from pots and pans, thread, ribbons and glass baubles to cough mixture, magical painkillers, and all manner of pills and potions to cure most of the ailments common to humanity. Quite a little crowd was gathered round him; he was always popular, and doing a good trade. When he spotted Priscilla he mouthed, 'Ten minutes', and signalled with two hands, managing to convey to her how long he'd be before giving her a lift back.

She nodded, and escaped into the fortune-teller's tent to avoid any chance of meeting with Jason again.

The woman inside was brown-skinned, oldish, with beady black eyes above a strong hawk nose and jutting chin. Brass rings dangled from her ears, glinting through straggling locks of greying hair. She was draped in a black shawl and seated on a steel before a small table with a crystal ball on it, and a pack of cards.

She peered at Priscilla shrewdly, beckoning her with a predatory bony finger.

'Come in, lady, and let Zillah cross your palm. A pretty palm it looks too, with much writ on it, I'll be bound. Take a seat now—' She indicated a second stool, on the opposite side of the table, to which Priscilla moved hesitantly.

'Sit thee down, lady,' the woman continued, 'and tell me – is it thy hand thee wants readin', or the cards?'

'My hand, I think,' Priscilla answered.

'Very well, then, and seein' as you're such a fine lady mebbe a coin first, eh? A coin so I knows you've a good heart, my dear, an' to bring us both luck.'

Knowing that heart didn't come into the business at all, but only greed, Priscilla nevertheless fished a sovereign from her reticule and handed it to the gipsy. Whether she was a true Romany or not was hard to tell, probably not, but some of the woman's comments as she studied the lines of the young, pale hand held by her own withered-looking brown one, came curiously near to the truth. The predictions ended in the usual way — 'However worried you be now, dear, in th' end the storm clouds'll clear, and you an' your true love will come together in the sunshine. But beware the dark man, lady — who wishes thee harm—'

Priscilla smiled ironically to herself as she left the tent. A dark man? Who could that be except Challoner, perhaps, and he had no personal grudge against her, nor was she likely to see him again since he was presumably still in foreign parts with Olivia.

Oh, it was all rubbish, and had been merely a matter of passing the time until Tommy's auction was over.

The small crowd round him was dispersing when she reached the cart and Tommy, well content, was packing the few remaining utensils unsold into the back of the cart, and getting the donkey ready for departure.

'I hope it's not taking you out of your way, getting me back to Mooncarn,' Priscilla said. 'Probably I could have transport from a farmer or Johnny Carne at the kiddleywink.'

'Now what would a fine young lady like you be needin' such as he to 'comp'ny thee, ma'am, when you c'n have old Tommy hisself? No, no. Tes all right. Come on, midear,' he gave a tug to her hand, 'up with ee. I'm goin' your way anyhow, as I did tell thee, straight on t'Penjust for the celebrations Monday mornin' when the circus arrives, an' t'collect bits an' pieces on the way.'

Priscilla hoisted herself as comfortably as she could into the small space beside Tommy, and moments later they were off. As they neared the stretch of lane above the spot where Lise had met her terrible death neither looked to right or left, but stared straight ahead as though no hungry sucking bog or malevolent influence had ever lingered there.

Back at Mooncarn, the full import of what had occurred between herself and Jason registered with renewed pain through Priscilla's whole being. Physically as well as emotionally and mentally she felt drained. During their fiery argument, her quick temper had obliterated commonsense and normal reasoning. Now she realised the stark truth of what she — or rather *they* — had done.

It really *was* over — finally, irrevocably. Even if she brought herself to plead with him, he would not forget her rash words, 'I hate you — hate.' Neither would he forgive her admittance that Alex had bought her. The lovely thing that had blossomed so briefly between them had died, through circumstance and her own wild nature.

And yet, she thought miserably, what she'd done for her father had seemed right at the time. If only Jason could have understood. If only — but there was no point in conjecturing. She still had Mooncarn, and the writing venture ahead, for what it was worth.

As things turned out it appeared that *Passionate Love*, or *The Adventures of Robert Tyzackass* was going to be worth quite a lot. During the following fortnight she received a letter of acceptance with an agreement from Blakey's publishing firm for the rights to produce her novel in its original form, simultaneously with a volume of her poems. The two books were scheduled to appear the following spring, and would be well promoted — especially the *Tyzackass* edition, which would have full advertisements proclaiming it was the genuine work of an eleven-year-old girl.

Priscilla, elated by the news, forgot briefly her personal unhappiness, caught up in a whirl of excited anticipation. It had happened at last; something she had written was going to appear in print. No one except Mrs James had *really* believed in her ability until then. But now they'd have to; even Alex.

Alex!

Her heart sank a little. Try as she would she could no longer accept they had any worthwhile future together.

This opinion was intensified by an unexpected visit from Alex himself during the following week. He looked contrite at first, perhaps even mildly ashamed, when he greeted her with forced sangfroid, in the hall, saying, 'Hullo there. Had to meet a fellow in Wynk, so thought I'd ride over just to see how you were getting on. Enjoying your little self?'

'I've got what I came for — peace and time to think,' Priscilla replied ambiguously. 'Are you staying for a cup of tea, Alex?'

'Tea? No thanks. I've a tot of something stronger in my pocket, and now I'm here I may as well empty it in your company. Where do we go? The lounge?'

'All right,' Priscilla agreed reluctantly.

Alex followed her into the newly decorated room and glancing round, remarked, 'Congratulations — you've spent the pater's little gift very tastefully.'

She flushed. 'Glad you approve.'

'Just so long as it doesn't become your headquarters,' he said meaningfully, though with still the tight little smile on his lips.

Priscilla studied him closely, wondering what he'd really come for, although she guessed it was to try and persuade her to return.

She was right; after a short discussion over everyday matters he said suddenly, 'When are you thinking of coming home, Prissy? My esteemed father wanted to know yesterday. I told him "quite soon". I hope I was right.'

Priscilla thought for a moment before answering. Then she told him in quiet level tones, 'No, I'm afraid not. I've — I've no intention of returning, Alex. I'm sorry — I mean I don't want to hurt your feelings, but—' She paused uncomfortably, aware how the unexpected statement must have shocked him; even she herself was surprised as the flat words left her lips. She hadn't intended to come to the point so quickly. Until the moment of her husband's entrance there'd been no clear-cut decision in her mind. But seeing him there, handsome in his riding kit — tentative and young-looking, yet behind the facade so sure of himself and her, so confident of her eventual compliance with his wishes — she'd known she must settle the matter there and then. She watched him frown, and stare at her in amazement; either she was playing with him, he thought, or had lost her reason.

'Don't be ridiculous,' he said. 'I asked you a sensible question.'

'And I've answered it. I don't want to — I don't see any point in delaying what's inevitable. We're not *suited*, Alex. And you must know that yourself by now. We haven't a thing in common

– not any more. I was fond of you as a friend, and I suppose—'
she shrugged, '—I suppose I imagined things would go on that
way – but—'

'Just pals, eh?' he interrupted sarcastically. 'With you getting
all the benefits on your side, and me nothing but the privilege of
forking out for your whims. No obligations whatever. Well – let
me tell you, my girl, you were wrong. And you're damn well
leaving Mooncarn the moment I say. You're my wife—' He
grabbed the bodice of her gown at its frilly neck and shook her.
'And it's going to remain that way, *Mrs* Stern.'

She flinched.

'Let me go. Or I'll—'

'Have me thrown out? Oh, I don't think so. The boot will be on
the other foot if it has to be. Mooncarn may be your property in
name, through the shortsightedness of my philanthropic papa –
but legally what is yours is mine, my dear. Remember that.'

He let go of her abruptly, his face white with only two spots of
colour staining his cheeks. She sat down, and he strode to the
window, stood there briefly, hands clenched at his side looking
out; then turned to face her again.

With an effort he said in more conciliatory tones, 'Prissy don't
be a fool. I've apologised already for that – that incident at the
Manor. I told you it wouldn't happen again. What more can I
do? Can't you believe it? Or is it that you want me to crawl at
your feet – because if so—'

'*No.*' Her voice was shrill. 'Of course I don't, and you
wouldn't do it, I know that. Anyway your "escapade",' her lip
curled, 'on the bed with Selina isn't really so important against
the rest. I'd have overlooked it in time, even forgotten it perhaps, if—'

'Yes, *if*—'

'If I'd loved you, Alex. But you see, I don't. And that's the
truth. Neither do you love me.'

'Thank you very much for putting words into my own mouth,
and for your very direct statement concerning your own feelings. If I remember correctly you gave quite a good imitation of
enjoying yourself in our own connubial sessions together—'

148

'I *tried* at first, because you and your father had been so nice about papa, and it seemed my duty.' Her tones faltered. 'I did *try*, Alex—'

'Oh, my God!'

He bowed his head, and covered his face with his hands.

'I'm sorry.' The apology issued only as a whisper from her. He glanced up again; his face had become hard, uncompromising.

'You're not getting out of things as easily as you seem to imagine,' he said at last, following a pause in which hatred seemed to come alive and intensify between them. 'If you really *mean* what you've said, and it's not just another of your dramatic episodes—'

'It isn't. I mean, I *do* mean it. Why would I *pretend* over such an important thing?'

'I don't know. I really don't. Unless — can it be there's another man? *Ah!* perhaps this retreat isn't such a virtuous little hidey-hole after all.'

She bit her lip, with the bright colour suddenly flooding her face.

'That's it, isn't it?' she heard him saying. 'A *lover*! and *you* — with the damned impudence to criticise me—' before she could avoid his upraised hand, he'd brought it sharply against her face. 'Well, madam — think about it. And before I leave, listen carefully — unless you're back at the Manor by the end of the month, I'll take action — somehow discover who he is, and ruin him. I'll file for divorce, and see you rue the day you thought to make a fool of me. *You*, and your *books*. You're nothing but a devious, scheming little bitch.'

He turned on his heel abruptly, and without another look at her slammed through the door, into the hall, and out of the front door.

Priscilla stood with a hand to her burning cheek. Ironically, she thought, how badly human beings could behave to each other, how uncivilized. An objective observer might have seen something mildly comic in the fact that she had raised her hand to Jason, just as Alex in his turn, had lifted his against *her*. She tried her best to view this latest incident of love's triangle in a light way, but failed dismally. As the last sight of her husband's figure faded down the drive, an unexpected welling of tears came to her eyes. But they did not fall. Hearing the girl coming along the passage she dabbed them hurriedly, assumed an air of confidence, and when the maid knocked said, 'Come in, Sally.'

The new girl appeared with a tray bearing the silver tea service, two bone china cups, saucers, and plates, with a dish of thinly cut sandwiches.

'Oh — the gentleman hasn't stayed, ma'am? I thought—'

'No. He only called to say how-do-you-do. Never mind. Put the tray down. Those sandwiches look very tempting.' What a lie — when she felt too sick at heart to eat a thing.

'Cress and egg, ma'am — and tomato. I was already arranging them when I heard him come. He didn't knock, so I thought he must be an old friend, and maybe like—'

'Yes, yes. Very considerate of you, Sally.'

'There's a cake, too, that cook made. But—'

'Oh, I won't need that,' Priscilla interrupted. 'And I shan't eat all these, but I'm sure they needn't be wasted.' For no reason at all she suddenly remembered how Mrs Jolly, her old dog who had died at a vast age only a year ago, had developed a passion for eggs, and dainty titbits from the table when she was a puppy. Yes, she decided suddenly, she must have a dog of her own at Mooncarn. The only one at present was the gardener's half-collie half-sheepdog, Rover, and he was a one-man pet.

Three days later she was about to visit Ned Craze at the farm concerning what breed he advised, when another unexpected visitor arrived at the house. From the doorway Priscilla saw he wore a brown top-coat with fawn trousers, a cream neck-scarf above a lemon waistcoat, and a tall beaver hat. He also carried a gold-knobbed cane. He was an elderly man, with pink cheeks emphasised by white sideburns. There was an air of importance about him as he alighted from a brougham, gave a few directions with a wag of a finger, and straightening himself, made decisively to the front door.

Priscilla felt her heart quicken with apprehension.

Lord Stern.

Whatever had *he* come for? To scold? Plead with her? Or to tell her Mooncarn was no longer hers? Surely not the latter. The place had been legally made over to her, not merely because she had wanted it, as his daughter-in-law, but also because of his friendship for her father. Unlike Alex, he was not petty-minded. And they had got on well together during the short time they'd really know each other.

Still, Alex was his heir, and heaven alone knew what tale he'd concocted about the recent meeting with her — his wife.

So she steeled herself to handle whatever situation arose with dignity, however difficult it proved to be.

As matters turned out the difficulties she'd half anticipated didn't arise.

Following a few preliminary remarks, the old man came straight to the point.

'Hear you two've been having troubles, you and that son of mine, eh?' He queried bluntly. 'Or has he exaggerated? You want to leave him, he says. Can't be right surely?'

'I — I'm afraid it is,' Priscilla answered, suddenly aware how inwardly upset her father-in-law was. 'It isn't that — I've nothing *against* Alex — except that—'

'The silly young rake felt like a bit of fun in bed with a house-maid, I know; — I *know*. And you felt ashamed, naturally. But — maybe you've taken it a bit too seriously. Eh? Oh, don't think I'm making excuses. Fact is, though, young men do run off the rails sometimes, and Alex was always spoiled.' He paused, but before Priscilla could say anything continued gruffly, 'His mother's fault. Even as a youngster he'd only have to shout for a thing and he got it. "Alicia," I told her time after time, "you'll be the ruin of that child. What he needs is a touch of the cane, instead of all that mollycoddling." But would she have it? *No*. And at Eton, of all places, it was the same story. Charm he had; and now see where it's got him.'

'I'm sure he'll get over it,' Priscilla said. 'And you're wrong — *partly*, anyway, about the — the frolic with Selina. I wouldn't let that alone spoil things between us. Lord Stern—' Her manner became more urgent, compelling his blue eyes under the bushy white brows to regard her more intently.

'Yes, m'dear?'

'It will be very hard to make you understand. But Alex and I – we don't think alike in any way at all. We haven't the same interests – we don't—'

'Come, come! it ain't *interests* that make a marriage, girl—'

She flushed. 'Not *only*, no. But the other thing—'

'Bed? Sex? Oh, excuse an old man for being blunt, but we've got to face facts. Are you trying to tell me that young Alex doesn't know how to prove himself a real husband, is that it?'

'*No.* He's quite adept.' In spite of herself she could not keep the irony out of her voice.

'Then what in the name of old Harry *is* wrong?'

'We don't get on. We just *don't get on*. It was all right when we were friends; but then we didn't know each other all that well then, did we? The decision to get married was very sudden; I had so many other things on my mind.'

'Hm! you mean your father.'

'Naturally. Although I wasn't just being mercenary, you know. I did *like* Alex, and I thought it would work. But it hasn't – and I know it never will. I'm so *sorry* – really I am—' She broke off, as disappointment, mingled with chagrin and annoyance flooded his face.

'And how do you think Clinton, your father, will take this damn-fool decision of yours?'

Her eyes were very clear, honest, and straight upon him, when she answered, 'I don't know.'

'Neither do I.'

'I hope you'll still – stand by him, that it won't make any difference to his future.'

'His future? He's settled now. You needn't fret about that. In any case Clinton and I get on, see things the same way. And I'm not the kind of man to desert a friend simply because his daughter turns out to be a pig-headed little fool.'

The interview continued for another five minutes with Lord Stern alternately pleading and letting off steam. At the end of it he asked without preamble, 'Have you a lover tucked away somewhere? Is that the real reason? Come along now, the truth.'

'No. I have no lover at present, Lord Stern. If I had I'd have told Alex. I'm not a hypocrite.'

'Well, that being so, I'm dumbfounded that's all — can't make head or tail of the situation. Not anyhow. But you just think over things, that's what I seriously advise you to do. Take time to see reason, because if you don't — then you may be sorry; very sorry indeed.'

They parted in a superficially amicable way, although Priscilla sensed beneath the bluff controlled exterior a deep sense of hurt and anger.

It was a few days later that something happened to sadden the meeting with Lord Stern temporarily to insignificance.

William had an accident.

8

William was astonished and upset when Lord Stern called at Seagrave Square to inform him of the impasse between his son and Priscilla.

'You must do what you can, William, to heal the breach,' he told his friend, shaking his head forbodingly. 'These things happen, we know, but when they do – in *our* circle—' meaning his own '—we generally turn a blind eye, hush 'em up – and accept them with a good grace. But a *real* scandal, a divorce, *unthinkable*. If that girl of yours means to throw her cap over the windmill she'll suffer for it in the end, mark my words. Young Alex hasn't committed a heinous crime, y'know. Try and talk sense into her, Will, eh? Be a good chap and put a stop to this ballyhoo before it blows up into public scandal. You know what newspapers are – one sniff, and up goes the social balloon.'

'I'll do what I can,' William answered with a sinking of his heart. 'But my daughter isn't easily manipulated. Once she sets her mind to a thing—'

'I thought she'd done that when she married my son. I *like* the girl – always did, was looking forward to her putting a grandson into my arms—' he sighed. 'But now it seems there's no chance of it – at the moment. Only for the moment, mind you. I refuse to believe your Prissy hasn't more sense in her head than to cause a serious rift in family relationships all because of a mood.'

William agreed in words and the matter was temporarily left there, but inwardly he was doubtful. He knew his daughter, and sensed that something far stronger than one misdemeanour from Alex had induced her to take such a strong stand. Her

154

writing? It *could* be, in part. But only, *only* part of the reason for her inexplicable behaviour. There must be a stronger force at work. The suggestion of a lover crossed his mind, as it had Stern's, but he vanquished it because he wanted to. He'd never been entirely rid himself of the niggling idea that in marrying young Alex she'd acted, whether wittingly or not, partly on his behalf.

He blamed himself for not having quizzed her more thoroughly concerning her true feelings for the young man. But the fact remained he'd been shocked, in the devil of a hole at the time, and the alliance had been the saving of his career and mental adjustment to his blindness.

Now, it seemed, *someone* had failed. Alex had been a fool, and Priscilla, for whatever reason, had decided she wanted no more of it.

Following Stern's departure, his anxiety increased.

The weather was humid and oppressive with the suggestion of a lowering mist hugging the square.

'Must get a breath of air,' he thought. 'Maybe a stroll round the gardens will freshen me up.'

He took his stick, pulled on a cape, and touching the flags every few yards or so with the cane, made his way down the hall and out of the side door. Usually he was steady on his feet, knowing every path of the garden well, and having adapted himself as successfully as possible through an additional sense of touch — in recompense for loss of vision.

That afternoon, however, he'd forgotten that changes were being made in certain paths bordering the rose and rock gardens, and with a sudden shock the toe of his boot stumbled against a piece of granite. His stick went flying, as he crashed forward, catching the side of his head against the hard surface of a broken paving stone. He fell sideways, saving harm to his face, but his head above one temple was badly bruised and cut. Hearing the crash a gardener came rushing from a nearby greenhouse, and after one look at the recumbent figure realised William was unconscious.

Help was summoned, a doctor was called who diagnosed concussion, an opinion later endorsed by a specialist.

For three days William lay in a coma, although his life was not feared for. Priscilla was sent for, and arrived at number 7 to find the house not wrapt in gloom, as she'd anticipated, but brought alive with excitement.

The master was recovering, she was told by the housekeeper, and best of all — only a few hours ago — he had regained his sight.

'A real miracle,' the kindly woman exclaimed. 'One moment the poor gentleman lying so still an' sick an' dead to the world, seemingly, the next, hearing his bell I arrive to see him suddenly sit up and say, "What the hell am I doing here? Where are my clothes?" Would you *believe* it, ma'am? After these months in a dark world — and so courageous he was — then, after a blow on the head — everything clear as day. Well, perhaps not *quite* clear, not yet. But the doctor says it'll come. Oh, ma'am — you should have seen his face when he realised. Of course, he's quietened down a bit now — I gave him something to calm him. But when he sees you—'

'Yes, yes. It *is* marvellous news, is he awake now?'

'He's having a cup of tea. So if you go up, he's in the study. The doctor says there's no reason why he shouldn't be about again properly in a few days fit as he ever was.'

Priscilla thanked her, and mounted the wide stairs leading to the front first floor portion of number 7 which had been left intact when alterations were made to house office staff.

The greeting between father and daughter was an emotional one in which Priscilla allowed no cloud of her own complicated domestic position to interfere with the relief and joy of finding her father able to communicate and observe and talk with her without the wearying business of pretence and acceptance of an existence which despite his outward pretexts had remained darkly within himself as a calamity.

She stayed at Seagrave Square for five days, and it was only towards the end of that period that William brought up the question of her relationship to Alex.

'Is it true that you want to leave him?' he queried on the spur of the moment when the conversation had somehow veered to

156

the amount of time she'd spent recently at Mooncarn. 'Stern was telling me you'd hinted you meant to bury yourself there and not return to Alex. I hoped he'd got it wrong.'

'No, he was right, papa,' Priscilla admitted. 'And I *did* mean it.'

'Hm. A pity.'

'I know. And it's my fault mostly, I suppose, for expecting him to be – well, different. I mean I'd always known – *you* must have done too – that he wasn't really the settling down kind.' She bit her lip, realising how old-fashioned she sounded, and before he could say more, continued quickly, 'That sounds ridiculous, doesn't it? Coming from me.'

'Yes.'

'The trouble really is that I don't love him sufficiently to put up with his weaknesses, or characteristics if you like,' she admitted, 'and the same goes for Alex. He resents my writing—'

'Ah! the publishing venture. Yes, Edward was telling me about it the other day. Must say, it came as quite a shock to me. A pleasant one, mind you – didn't realise I'd a genius for a daughter.'

'Oh, not a *genius*, papa, but it's exciting, and makes me feel sort of fulfilled.'

'But, my dear girl, fulfilment for a woman means something more than that. Jove, yes. Having a family, being a mother and wife – those are the things that count in the long-run. You mark my words, writing books is all right as a side-line, if you're lucky enough to get anyone to publish them, but beyond that – oh, come *on*, Prissy, have sense. Use your brain, girl, and see what you already have in your marriage. Romance doesn't last f'r ever you know, as I found out to my cost. And whatever you may believe I'd stake my life on the fact that Alex'll never give a serious thought to another woman whilst he has you.'

Priscilla suddenly gave her father a look so stubborn, so direct, that he *knew*, without being told, his argument counted for nothing.

'And what about *me*?'

'You?'

'Yes, *me*, papa.'

He screwed up his eyes which were tiring slightly, before replying, 'I don't know what you mean.'

'No. And it's better you shouldn't.'

'For heaven's sake, girl—'

'Papa—' her voice and expression betrayed an inner distress that daunted him, '—please let's leave talking about Alex and me,' she continued, 'one day perhaps I'll be able to explain better, and maybe you'll be able to understand. I do hope so. But it's no use at the moment.' She turned from him and stood with her back rigid, head high, staring through the window at the gently swaying branches of the trees in the garden.

'All right, girl,' she heard William saying presently, 'don't worry, I'll not fret you again with questions. But for your own sake, think well before you do anything rash. Just wait. Leave things over for a time. I'm not entirely an old fool, Prissy, and I can't believe that this sorry affair is one-sided. I'm a builder, remember? And triangles sometimes have a nasty habit of causing more trouble than's expected. Remember that.'

The memory of Jason had occurred to him like a bolt from the blue; he hoped he was wrong, but a niggling sense of putting two and two together told him he was right.

Jason Blakey was somehow deeply involved in Priscilla's heart.

*

The celebration party to mark the publication of Cornelia Almond's novel *The Adventures of Robert Tyzackass* — the title finally decided upon — was arranged by the publishers for a day in late April 1859, at a fashionable London restaurant of the period — the glamorous L'Epicure. Priscilla, thrilled and excited by the prospect, was also apprehensive. She would much have preferred a smaller, more private affair at Seagrave Square, but Edward Blakey remained firm on the point.

'The luncheon will be an important part of the promotion,' he said, 'including as well your poems. The guests have been carefully chosen, with a number of helpful Press Representatives. My dear, we want as large a coverage as possible. With proper handling your *Robert Tyzackass* should be a sell-out before it appears on the bookshelves. And by then, remember, you will not merely be the titillating child authoress of a 'most amusing and dramatic' piece of fiction, but Priscilla Stern, daughter of William Clinton, now grown up, the wife of Lord Stern's son, Alex, also a poetess of considerable potentiality.'

'Oh, but—' Priscilla's intended protest was interrupted by one of Edward's business cronies, and shelved for the time being.

She returned to Mooncarn two days later, having chosen her outfit for the occasion, a sophisticated but feminine two-piece in shot-silk taffeta verging from sea-green to pastel blue and a small perched forward hat with a shred of veiling behind.

She had it sent to Mooncarn so she could be certain of her choice, and could try it on at least without the costumier's string of high-flown adjectives and compliments. The few servants there were enthusiastic and the housekeeper's comments, though restrained were flattering.

'Yes. You look really charming, ma'am. Nothing too outrageous about it. It has the look of the sea and soft sunshine, somehow. Oh, you'll charm everyone.'

Priscilla naturally was pleased, but also sad that the one person, Jason, whose opinion would have meant so much would not be there to give it.

She'd learned from Edward that he was on the high seas somewhere, and not expected back in Britain before June.

If Edward knew anything of the affair between his brother and Priscilla she didn't know, but felt it was hardly likely.

However, a fortnight before her return to Plynport, in order to prepare for the luncheon, Edward arrived himself at Mooncarn, looking serious and somewhat disturbed.

When they were ensconced alone together in the lounge, and after the first perfunctory greetings were over, he produced a wellknown London daily paper that ran one of the most sensational gossip columns in the country.

'I think you should read it, Priscilla,' he said, handing it to her. 'It could be important at this juncture. We have sufficient time — *just* — to issue a denial, if the rubbish is untrue, and if you agree, which I'm sure you will.'

Bewildered, Priscilla took the paper from him, and under the heading 'LORD'S SON ABOUT TO SUE FOR DIVORCE?' read:

It is rumoured in well-known social circles that the Honourable Alex Stern is about to sue for divorce from his young wife, who before her marriage was Priscilla Clinton, daughter of William Clinton, the famous engineer and architectural contractor. The news, if true, is doubly interesting, since Mrs Stern has been discovered to be the authoress of a book about to be published *The Adventures of Robert Tyzackass*, which was written when she was an unknown child prodigy of only eleven years. Seeds of romance evidently must already have been thriving in this precocious young lady's heart, and it would be interesting if any contemporary Tyzackass were found to be hovering somewhere in the background. At her Cornish retreat? Or is the story merely a myth? Whatever the truth, the novel is bound to create interest among critics and the public alike.

After reading the paragraph not only once but twice, Priscilla stared at Edward incredulously.

'How *dare* they? Who on earth wrote this — this rubbish?'

'That's what I'd like to know — what *every*one involved with the publication would like to know,' Edward told her gravely.

'But it's — it's *libellous*, isn't it?'

Edward shrugged. 'The words aren't quoted as *fact*, simply rumour; and whether they'd be actionable is doubtful. It would depend rather on whether or not there's any truth in the suggestion.'

Priscilla felt the colour flooding her face. 'How do *I* know?' she remarked abruptly, turning her eyes away from his, and fiddling nervously with the ivory brooch at her throat.

'But — you're surely the only one who does, apart from Alex?'

When she didn't reply, he continued, 'I'd no idea there was anything questionable about your relationship with your

160

husband. The reason for your presence so frequently here — at Mooncarn — was taken by me, to ensure you had peace for your work — your writing — that there was a more serious cause never entered my head. So far, all the publicity and advertisements given to the press by our firm, have portrayed you as an enterprising happy young couple — and yourself as a first-class example of a married woman successfully combining a career with the normal duties of a wife.'

'Yes.'

The flat acceptance of his statement took Blakey aback. It was obvious to him from her curt manner that the tit-bit of social trash might, after all, come very near the truth.

'I must ask you,' he said coldly, 'to be straight with me about things. Are you and young Stern separated?'

'I've left him, and I'm not going back,' Priscilla admitted. 'About the divorce business — I don't know. I really don't. Alex did threaten it if I wouldn't return to him, but at the time I didn't really believe it.'

'Has he a case? A just cause? Sorry to sound pedantic, Priscilla, but you must know what I mean? Is there another man?'

Then she dropped her bomb-shell.

'Yes, Mr Blakey. But I've only seen him once since I married Alex. And there's been no — adultery — that's the word, isn't it?'

Edward inclined his head.

'May I enquire who?'

'You may enquire, but I'd rather not tell you. Since we're hardly likely to meet again — in the near future anyway — I don't see the name's important.'

He didn't press the point. With shrewd insight he guessed the third party might easily be his brother. Though Jason had never admitted or hinted to him of a serious involvement with Clinton's daughter, Edward had sensed Jason's quickened interest whenever her name was mentioned between them. Perhaps, if the two of them, Jason and himself — had met more frequently the younger man might have confided something of his feelings where the girl was concerned — if any. But their careers and life-styles were so different and apart they hardly met, except for special occasions and as time went by such contacts became more rare.

Edward was frankly worried, and told Priscilla so.

'For the sake of the firm, your book, and for a pleasant public image, wouldn't it be possible for you to soothe your husband down temporarily — present an acceptable facade of unity for the time being?' he asked hopefully. 'It would go a long way towards getting a sound readership. The Directors of Blakey's and myself have gone to considerable expense in backing the novel, and the picture of a young future divorcee having written such a naively innocent piece of fiction is going to detract from a sense of authenticity. The magazines won't like it, the critics will give sly comments in no way very helpful. As a favour now—' he broke off, frustrated by the sudden helpless look of confusion — of distress on Priscilla's face. Her beautiful eyes held an anguish which seemed to him out of all proportion to the occasion, important as it was to him and the firm.

'Oh, Mr Blakey — Edward — you've been so good to me, and it's hateful feeling I've let you down. I wish now — I wish I'd never *thought* of *Robert Tyzackass*. And now you've made him very important I don't know how to deal with it — all that's happened since, I mean. I didn't realise there'd be so much publicity, or that I'd have to be written about and photographed and promoted — don't you *see*? It's not *me*. And how could I *pretend* to be in love with Alex when our life's impossible? — I *couldn't*. It would make me feel *cheap* somehow. And anyway everyone will know in time, won't they — when it — *if* it happens, the divorce, I mean?'

'I suppose so. I was hoping for a denial from you, followed by a stiff letter to the paper and a demand for an instant apology. But after what you've just told me the only course left to us, I suppose, is to appear to ignore the statement and hope things will be allowed to rest there. However—'

'Yes?'

'You may or may not know that your husband has already been invited to the luncheon. An influential director of Blakey's happened to be a friend of Lord Stern's and a fellow club member. Naturally it's to be hoped there'll be no obvious show of antagonism between you and your husband, *should* he appear.'

Priscilla's finely moulded profile took its upward characteristically proud thrust. 'I shan't create a scene, if that's what you fear. So long as Alex doesn't make a show of himself, I'll do my best to behave properly.'

Edward, realising he could hope for no more from the interview, left a little later, worried still and quite aware that during the next few days other periodicals sensing a good storyline, might take up the unsavoury gossip paragraph, making far more of it than was fact, and that there was nothing he could do about it without Priscilla's help — the help she refused to give.

*

There were many times during the following week, when Priscilla seeking wildly for an excuse not to appear at the London luncheon, wondered whether it would be possible to plead some disability — illness, a heavy cold — or even an accident of some kind — a badly twisted or broken ankle — any white lie to save her from the disagreeable and embarrassing situation of having to face Alex in public. Very possibly — hopefully, he wouldn't turn up. But knowing his likeness for odd situations she knew it was quite likely that he would, if even to unnerve and upset her. And his mood had been aggressive lately in the letters he'd sent to her.

Firmly she kept her mind away from Jason, but sometimes, when the sighing of the wind outside whispered through the heather and gorse, and ships' sirens moaned from the distant sea, his image returned to haunt her. Whenever she took a stroll by moors or along the cliffs, her heart would instinctively quicken with a sense that he might suddenly appear round a bend or rocky turning of land. The air was heady those days with the wild sweet scents of spring and pale thrusting undergrowth. Blossom foamed against paperclear skies, birds chortled from their nests, and young lambs frisked in the stone-walled fields. The primroses were profuse and thick, spreading a golden carpet by ditches and hedgerows.

All life seemed to be waking and thriving with the hope of adventure and fruition ahead. At intervals she allowed herself to be possessed by life's verdant promise, dismissing her disastrous marriage as a mere incident that her imagination refused to accept as reality. She became, then, a creature of the elements — of wind, sea, sun, racing clouds and rain — unfettered and free — a child of the moors and the wild sweet passion first kindled by Jason to whom she'd sworn fidelity, standing with him by the great stones of the open hills.

Oh, this surely was her true self — this self who'd dreamed and created romantic visions when she was a child — the self she still remained at heart, and would be forever. Only through love of her father had she betrayed it — and surely she couldn't be blamed for that. Surely life would provide her escape from the bondage of duty and respectability.

Duty? What duty could there be to Alex, when he threatened the very essence of her heart and soul? Or was that being melodramatic, perhaps? It was so easy to let her thoughts, feelings, even words, get out of control.

In quieter moments, when her senses had cooled and she could think clearly, she accepted that her publishers *did* have a certain claim on her behaviour. They had spent time and money on her, and shown confidence in her talents and creative ability. So she would not let them down. She would appear at the luncheon given in her honour, and act with all the pride and dignity she could muster, giving the press, and any nosy journalist present, no chance to print snide or derisive comments later.

The only point on which she would not compromise was her decision never to return to Alex.

9

Priscilla joined William at Seagrave Square for four days before journeying to London for the luncheon at L'Epicure. She found her father in cheerful spirits, a little more portly and with an occasional screwing up of his eyes which denoted a nervous tension as though he could not yet fully accept he could really see again. His hair had more grey in it, and his complexion was a little more ruddy. Otherwise he seemed the ebullient creative character she'd known since childhood, and full of plans concerning a new building site on the outskirts of the city for which he'd obtained the contract.

Only twice did he refer to the scandalmongering concerning her life with Alex, which had appeared in certain malicious newspaper columns. 'Take no notice,' he said. 'The yellow press. That's what they call it. What they don't know they make up.'

'Yes, I suppose so,' Priscilla had agreed the first time, with a thin smile on her face.

'You *suppose*? It's not true, is it, girl?'

'Only that we're separated. *That* is. But you already knew that didn't you? As for the rest—' she shrugged. 'Well — it's all just *hints*, isn't it? And you know me, papa. I won't be dictated to by any nosy newspaper or stuffy magazine about how I should live. I said as much to Edward. He didn't like it, I'm afraid, but he's a serious sort of person underneath his charm. I didn't realise before. The man who came to preach at me at Mooncarn was completely different from the one I danced the polka with at my birthday affair. They're not a bit alike are they — he and — Jason?'

William had glanced at her face, then quickly away. Her

165

expression was so suddenly softened and vulnerable. There was no longer any need to probe and conjecture. What he'd feared was true. She was in love with the young adventurer, and Prissy never loved lightly. A sigh had escaped him, because he realised there'd be difficulties ahead.

For the time being, however, he did his best to push all forebodings from his mind, and at the appointed time set off with his daughter by steam-train for London.

They stayed at an hotel in the West End, near Hyde Park, which was conveniently situated not far from L'Epicure. The weather was fresh and fine, free of any sign of rain or threat of fog which could be so disrupting to London traffic. For two days before the event Priscilla had opportunities to do necessary shopping, watch riders in The Row, and disport herself in the elegant new outfits brought for the occasion. In the company of William she visited Sydenham Hill to view the amazing Crystal Palace which had been removed there from Hyde Park in 1852 following the Great Exhibition of 1851. A trip to Kew was arranged, and Hampton Court. She was so diverted during those hours spent with her father that the shadow of Jason, and her apprehension of the event ahead, emerged only very occasionally to discomfort her.

William was relieved to see her so apparently carefree and happy, although he did venture to remark once, 'It isn't me who should be escorting you about, you know. Wish you could have found it possible to make up with young Alex. His father's distressed – expected me to do something about it. The old boy's wounded, Prissy, and you can't blame him.'

'I don't, papa. But I'm quite sure he'll soon get over it and be grateful to me in the end.'

'Grateful?'

She nodded. 'When Alex really accepts I never mean to live with him again, he'll soon find someone else – some girl with a handle to her name probably, and the capacity to fortify the Stern family tree with lots of little Sterns. A breeder of sons. That's what Lord Stern wants – *and* Alex. Oh, he'll come round, papa, in time.'

'Which means there *will* be a divorce.'

'I suppose so.'

'Prissy—'

'Dear papa, don't spoil things, *please*. I know I must be a worry to you. But it *is* my life.'

He patted her hand, knowing further talk was useless. Well, he'd done his best. Priscilla was a character, a true Clinton, and young Alex hadn't been man enough to keep her; that's what the whole sorry business amounted to. Good luck to her then, and to Jason Blakey, if he was the one she really wanted. The last thing he wished to do was to stand in the way of his girl's happiness.

'So it is, so it is,' he said, in answer to her statement. 'We'll forget the pother then, and get on with living. Don't worry, love, I'll not bring the matter up again.'

His tone and manner had been deliberately cheerful, but beneath the facade apprehension gnawed at him. And as things turned out, not without cause.

Next morning was the day of the book launching celebration where doubts and misgivings proved to be well-founded, though no-one would have guessed in what way. Certainly not William Clinton or Lord Stern.

*

Throughout the whole proceedings of the luncheon, Priscilla had a confused heady impression of flowers, crowds, of bonnets, curls, warm air mingled with the smell of perfume and wine, of muffled voices followed by applause, toasting, the clink of glasses, and sudden silences between speeches through which the name of Tyzackass vaguely registered. Waiters moved soundlessly over thick carpets, between small tables exotically decorated by unique flower arrangements. Silk rustled, colours of feminine gowns glowed beneath subtle lighting which blended the darker shades of male attire into a muted pattern of light and shade.

The guests comprised a number of the editorial and artistic fraternity, a few influential business associates, and one or two

167

of the nobility. Priscilla, at intervals, was aware of individual faces watching her, both male and female. Of the latter, one in particular caught her attention from time to time — a dead white face with scarlet lips under a mane of yellow hair crowned by a small black hat swathed in veiling, to match the rest of her sombre but elegant attire. Her eyes seemed to be on Priscilla constantly, watchful, secretive eyes holding perhaps jealousy? Who was she? Someone of importance, probably, Priscilla decided. Or was it she herself — Cornelia Almond, the potential celebrity — who was in some way out of gear, unequal to the occasion.

A kind of panic rose in her. She felt smothered, somehow out of place and provincial in her new well-cut outfit which had seemed so exactly right before this ridiculous — yes, it really *was* ridiculous — toasting to the success of *Sir Robert Tyzackass* started. Tyzackass did not belong here; he was a creature of her imagination — of the moors and seas and secret coves of the Cornish coast. Feeling slightly giddy, she gripped the edge of the table to steady herself as Edward's voice silenced the gathering, and with glass held aloft, announced, 'To our new authoress, Miss Cornelia Almond, and the success not only of her youthful romance *The Adventures of Sir Robert Tyzackass*, but of her fine adult volume — *Poems of Purity and Passion*.'

'Hear, hear!' came muffled applause accompanied by the clinking of glasses. The murmuring continued, but Priscilla did not hear it, for the door at the far end of the room suddenly swung open and through the blurred haze of movement and slowly dying down of conversation, a figure lurched — that of a man conventionally and elegantly attired, but obviously worse for drink, and oblivious to the demands of conventional behaviour.

Alex.

Priscilla's heart lurched as he wove his way between the tables, half-stumbling, knocking two over with a rattle of tumbled crockery, silver and glass, before anyone had time to stop him. His cravat was loose, his hair tumbled over one eye, and at every second or two he raised an arm shouting, 'There she is – the – the trollop – my *wife* – d'you hear? Tha'ss – tha'ss her – tha'ss the one—' he waved a fist towards Priscilla, while Edward got to his feet beside her. 'An' tha'ss him – his *brother*'s the one – I *know*, d'you hear? I've proof of it – the bloody slut—' by then waiters and others were trying with difficulty to restrain him. But Alex still fought, kicking and struggling. From the back somewhere Lord Stern made his way outraged and shaking towards his son.

'What the devil do you mean by this?' he shouted, 'Appearing like any drunken oaf from the gutter – a son of *mine*, a *Stern*. By God, I'll have no more of it, get up and out, sir, before I tackle you meself. A disgrace you are – a buffoon—'

A quality in the old man's voice – something familiar must have registered through Alex's befuddled brain; he blinked, sagged fell, and was then dragged unceremoniously from the scene, head lolling loosely on his breast.

Turmoil followed.

Priscilla's sight dimmed. Feeling sick and faint she managed to get to her feet, and before attention was once more turned on her, plunged through the crowd, running heedlessly out of the door and along the corridor – as she thought – to the ladies' dressing room.

But she had miscalculated.

With a shock, not entirely unpleasant, she felt a rush of fresh air brush her face, and found herself on the top step of the outer entrance leading into the street. She had a vague recollection of a liveried footman offering a supporting hand but instead she went on, to land up in a gentleman's arms, and held there firmly against his chest.

'I'm sorry – oh, I really am. I—' she tried to free herself, but couldn't. Against her ear she heard a dimly recognisable voice murmuring, 'Thy coach be waiting for thee, Cinderella. Sir Robert Tyzackass at thy service. Allow me—' she was unceremoniously pulled, half-carried along the pavement to a cab waiting nearby, pushed in, and flung down upon the seat, followed by her captor. There was a word of command to the driver, a flick of a whip, and the vehicle started off with the clip-clop of horses' hooves quickening to a steady pace in a direction eastwards from L'Epicure.

For seconds she was too bewildered, shocked, and out of breath to speak, or even have a clear glance at her companion's face. When she did, the confusion of her emotions — relief, outrage, amazement intermingled with a queer sense of humour, forced her only to collapse against the back of the cab, exclaiming, 'Jason! — *Jason!* How could you?' And then she started to laugh.

'Is that all the thanks I get for rescuing you from a *very* tricky situation?' Jason enquired. 'It seemed *most* apt to me. I apologise for my cravat, and for this damned hair of mine which behaves as badly as any unruly young woman.'

'But how did you — how did you *know*?' she asked. 'What would happen, I mean? — that Alex was going to make a scene? You had this cab waiting — or — or hadn't you?'

'Oh, yes, it was waiting. But only for the time taken by Alex to barge in. I waited to see what happened.'

His arm tightened round her waist. Her figure sagged against him, head on his shoulder, with the absurd little hat fallen crushed from its strings and her hair tumbled from its combs and pins.

'Were you with him then?' she queried quietly.

'Shsh?' he put a finger to his lips. 'Wait until we get to the Silver Fox, and I'll explain.'

'Where's that? The Silver Fox?'

'An inn I know. Quite a respectable place — in spite of its locality.'

'But you can't — I mean *I can't*,' she exclaimed suddenly pulling herself away. 'There's my father and Edward and Lord Stern — they'll all be worried. I shall be missed. Oh, Jason!' She sat up very straight and surveyed him with a hint of temper in her eyes — 'This is *abduction*. Do you *realise*? And after that last time we met when I slapped your face—'

'And I threatened a spanking?' he laughed abruptly. 'Yes, you were quite a little termagant. However — much as you may hate me, and I deplore your stubborn wayward mind — oh, Prissy, I love you so much.'

170

She sighed with a deep contentment spreading through her, then she remarked, 'You haven't answered my question. What about papa and the others—?'

'When we get to the inn, you'll write a note informing your papa and the noble Stern fraternity that you're safe and well in my company, and happy. The letter will be delivered by hand immediately either by an acquaintance of mine at the hostelry, or by some jarvey — maybe this one who will be well paid — to William Clinton, c/o L'Epicure. Now, for the moment, Prissy, please close your pretty mouth and leave the probing till later. It's confounded difficult answering questions to the accompaniment of horses' hooves and carriage wheels. On top of which I *am* slightly disorientated.'

'I don't believe *that* for one moment.'

'Then don't, my love. Just relax and trust me.'

Something in his voice at that moment impelled her to obey. She sat back and gradually the wild beating of her heart eased to a steady rhythm as buildings and streets became darker and more mean looking, and narrow cobbled byways criss-crossed the main thoroughfares of shabby buildings interspersed with markets and huddled factories.

The Silver Fox stood on the outskirts of London's dockland. It was an ancient low-roofed building, probably originating from the Elizabethan period, with a bar, tap room, a coffee lounge, catering for travellers of varying social class. Jason was obviously on good terms with the landlord, who instantly directed them to a small private interior, where paper, ink, and a quill pen were provided for Priscilla's use.

At Jason's dictation, with a few added comments of her own, she informed William that she had decided not to return to Seagrave Square, she was with Jason, who would take good care of her, and when she had a clear picture of what she was going to do in the future she would inform him instantly.

Please — *please* don't worry, dear papa! [she added as a postscript]. I realise Lord Stern and Edward will think I've behaved badly. But you must admit Alex was *quite revolting*

171

— and I know you wouldn't wish me to waste my time trying to be a good wife to him. There will be a scandal, of course, but there'd have been one anyway — I only hope, for Edward's and the publisher's sakes, sales of the Tyzackass book won't be affected. My love as ever, and if you feel like it tell Alex I bear him no ill-will — in fact, I'm doing him a favour in providing him with evidence for such an easy divorce. Affectionately, once more, your loving daughter,

> Prissy.

Jason read the note, folded and slipped it in an envelope, then handed it to the waiting cabby who after more generous remuneration than ever anticipated took it off forthwith and at full speed to L'Epicure.

'And now,' said Priscilla, 'perhaps you really will put me in the picture, Jason. I think you owe it to me, don't you?'

'Not really, my love. The debts between us are pretty well evened out, I think. Still, since you're such a one for words, the explanation, for what it's worth, is simple.

'I worked devilish hard to get ashore in time for your — celebration. It was touch and go; never mind, I did it. Rather late, but no matter. When I got out of the cab I spotted Alex swaying about on the steps of that place — L'Epicure, so I told the cabby to wait a bit, until I'd either got him properly on his feet or persuaded him to take a ride somewhere and sober up. But would he have it? Good heavens no. He was far too drunk and started shouting and lunging out at me as though I was "old Harry" come to molest him. Twice I got him upright. Then I got a blow on his chin. I was about to knock him out when I thought of you. "What the hell!" I told myself. "If I drag him inside and Edward sees me, he'll imagine the worst — think there's been a shindy of my making between us. His Lordship and her papa will naturally blame me, and Prissy'll be in the deuce of a difficult situation. So let him go, and I'll wait. Maybe she'll need me".'

He paused before adding, 'And you did, didn't you?'

Priscilla stared at him, intense, and very clear-eyed. Then she said, 'I've always needed you, Jason. I think I always will.'

'As much as you need Tyzackass?'

She laughed softly.

'Oh, Tyzackass is just part of me. Anyway — he'll be finally written off now, won't he? I mean when all this comes out the book won't have a chance, and I just *don't care* one bit.'

'To the contrary, sweetheart, you'll find booksellers and the public clamouring to have copies for their shelves. Mark my words — *Sir Robert Tyzackass* is about to make a first impact on the literary — or should we say — reading world — quite dramatic. I know you've never sought publicity, Priscilla, but darling, you happen to be the type of young woman who just can't avoid it. You wait and see.'

Still in a whirl, Priscilla had to accept Jason's story, although she discovered that any period of waiting, for the moment, was nil. Jason's wild unpredictable action of sweeping her from the restaurant to the musty small parlour of the old inn — though exciting and a relief — had nevertheless plunged her into an atmosphere of unreality in which confused thoughts whirled through her brain at such speed she felt lost, in a limbo of uncertainty that made her wonder momentarily if it was true or if she'd waken presently in her old bedroom at Seagrave Square, or at Mooncarn. The smell of malt and smoke permeating the air, the constant drone of conversation from the adjoining taproom and bursts of sudden hilarity emphasised the sense of being in another world — another sphere of existence. Only Jason seemed real to her — the one anchor she could cling to for guidance.

She was tired, of course. The wine, the party, and Alex's insufferable behaviour, could explain the exhaustion now encompassing her. But Jason seemed so confident — so certain that his plans for them both would work, and were *right*. 'New Zealand,' she heard him say in a daze at one point. 'That's where we're bound for, love — I've work to do there — a study of the flora and fauna, and lives of the inhabitants — the Maoris, so Edward can have a book which is a firsthand record of the place. The weather's superb there, I've heard. Of course, we won't be rich, but I've enough for us to get by on, and when we

173

come back in eighteen months' time – maybe two years – the scandal will've died down, and society will lay the red carpet for Jason Blakey and his lovely wife, the famous authoress of *The Adventures of Sir Robert Tyzackass*—'

'But Jason – *Jason*—' Priscilla managed to interrupt, 'what about Alex, and the divorce? And my father, and – and—'

'Yes?'

'Oh, *everything*. You're going so fast, I just can't keep up with you. You're taking everything for granted. New Zealand! How do you know I want to go there?'

The elation left his face. He thought for a moment and then said unexpectedly, 'You're quite right, I *don't* know. I can only hope. And I can't promise it will be easy there. It won't be, not all the time. Maybe I shouldn't have assumed so much. But time's so short, Prissy. I have to sail tonight—'

'*Tonight?*'

He nodded. 'My ship's out there in the estuary, waiting. A fine craft. Fit for our first home together, love – think of it – open skies, sea, sun, rain – and you and I, pioneers in a way—' His blue eyes blazed. 'There'll be good days, and difficult ones, but a new land ahead. Oh yes. Maybe even a new life if we choose to stay there. What do you say? Tell me, but think hard first. Think hard, and fast. Be *sure*, Prissy. That's important. The one thing that really matters. Otherwise,' he shrugged. '—I'll have to take off alone. But only half of me will be there – the hard part.'

How absurd, she thought, through her bewilderment, to expect her to make such a hasty decision. As for being *sure*! – the very floor of the room, the walls, and ceiling seemed to sway uncertainly round her. If she'd been the fainting sort she'd have swooned. But she wasn't. She closed her eyes momentarily, gripping the sides of her chair. Then she got up and said very clearly, though her lips were trembling, 'Let us make a start then. I'll go with you, Jason. As soon as you like.'

An exclamation of joy and triumph broke from him. He strode towards her and crushed her body against his, with his mouth soft, yet so firm and hard on her lips, she could neither move nor properly get her breath.

'Oh, Jason – Jason—' she tried to cry protestingly, but the words became mere gasps of sound. Then, suddenly, he released her.

'Right. Then off we go. Come along, love. Time to eat and drink later when we're properly on course.'

A haze was thickening when they reached the docks, and half an hour later Jason and Priscilla stood hand in hand watching the coast of Britain gradually taken into uniformity with sea and sky, until it eventually faded altogether, leaving only the open ocean before and round them, with a few gulls wheeling overhead.

EPILOGUE

Extract from a London newspaper, 1862

Mr Jason Blakey, the explorer, returned to London yesterday with his wife, Mrs Priscilla Blakey, daughter of William Clinton, the noted builder and engineer. As Cornelia Almond she became famous for her novel *The Adventures of Sir Robert Tyzackass*, written when she was a child.

Mr Blakey has new and outstanding information concerning Britain's important colony which is to be published later in a book produced by his brother, Edward Blakey, head of the family firm in Vigo Street.

Mrs Blakey was formerly married to the present Lord Stern, whose father died twelve months ago from a stroke. The marriage was dissolved in 1860.

Asked if the couple intended to make their permanent home in New Zealand, Mr Blakey replied in the affirmative, but also revealed that he hoped he and his wife would spend some months of most years at their Cornish retreat of Mooncarn in this country.